D0667559

THE GIRLS GET EVEN

● ● ● ● ●

Also by Phyllis Reynolds Naylor:

THE WITCH'S EYE
WITCH WEED
THE WITCH RETURNS
THE BOYS START THE WAR

THE GIRLS GET EVEN

Phyllis Reynolds Naylor

Delacorte Press

J
N333gi

Published by
Delacorte Press
Bantam Doubleday Dell Publishing Group, Inc.
1540 Broadway
New York, New York 10036

Library of Congress Cataloging in Publication Data

Naylor, Phyllis Reynolds.
    The girls get even / by Phyllis Reynolds Naylor.
        p.   cm.
    Summary: As Halloween approaches, the three Malloy sisters find themselves continually trying to get even with the four Hatford brothers, who have been playing tricks on them since the Malloys moved from Ohio to West Virginia. Sequel to "The Boys Start the War."
    ISBN 0-385-31029-3
    [1. Brothers and sisters—Fiction. 2. Revenge—Fiction. 3. Halloween—Fiction.] I. Title.
    PZ7.N24Gi   1993
    [Fic]—dc20   92-43047
                                                      CIP
                                                       AC

Manufactured in the United States of America

October 1993

10   9   8   7   6   5   4   3   2   1

BVG

*To the students of East Main Street School and
Buckhannon-Upshur Intermediate School in
Buckhannon, West Virginia,
which is almost, but not quite,
where this story
takes place*

Contents

· · · · ·

THE GIRLS GET EVEN

● ● ● ● ●

One

•

Making Plans

"Wait till Halloween!"

That was the battle cry these days, except that neither Caroline nor her sisters were sure exactly how Halloween would change things. No matter what they thought of to get even, there were always tricks the boys might play on them that would be far worse.

Caroline could not get it out of her mind. Her fingers were still sore from peeling all those apples for Mrs. Hatford, because Mrs. Hatford thought that's what Caroline had come over to do. And if Caroline had told her that the boys had locked her in their shed, she would have had to explain why she'd been over there spying on them in the first place.

And if she'd said she'd been trying to catch Wally Hatford doing something embarrassing so she could humiliate him the way he had humiliated her, she would have had to explain what had happened before that, and then before that, all the way back to when the Malloys had moved to Buckman in August and the Hatford boys had tried to drive them out. It was just too complicated, and neither her parents nor the boys' parents would stand for such nonsense one moment if they knew.

What their parents didn't understand was that Caroline and her sisters could no more go without getting even than they could go without breathing. In fact, half the fun of getting even was to see what the boys would think up next, just so Caroline, Beth, and Eddie could "get even" all over again. They'd never had so much excitement back in Ohio.

"You know," Mother said at breakfast that Saturday, "I'm beginning to love living in a big old house like this. If we move back to Ohio, Ralph, I think we should build an addition onto that house."

"We'll see," Coach Malloy murmured, munching his toast over NFL ratings in the paper.

Caroline exchanged helpless looks with her two older sisters. *If we move back to Ohio . . . ?* There was still the possibility that Dad would go back to his old coaching job there? As much as Caroline had hated the thought of moving to West

Virginia in the first place, she now desperately wished to stay.

Where else would they find a group of ready-made rivals just their ages? Where else would they live on a road called Island Avenue? The large piece of land in the middle of Buckman was not really an island, because it was surrounded on only three sides by water, but people called their road "Island Avenue" anyway. If you were coming into town on Island Avenue, you kept going until you were out on the very tip, and then you crossed the bridge over into the business district. You might not even have noticed that the river on your right was the same river that was on your left; it simply looped about at the end of the island.

This little college town had everything that their home back in Ohio did not—even a swinging footbridge across the river connecting them to the college campus and the street that led to the school. Caroline, who was only eight but was in fourth grade because she was precocious, dreamed of being an actress someday. And when she saw the river, the footbridge, the large old house they would live in, and the old school with a real stage and velvet curtain, she knew that this was the place she would make her debut.

•

Caroline was standing in front of the mirror in her room, her long thick ponytail tucked up under one of her mother's hats—the navy-blue hat with a veil that Mother reserved for funerals. She was pretending to be the wife of a captain who had been drowned at sea. She was practicing going from sad to grief-stricken to hysterical when she heard Eddie, the oldest, clattering up the stairs.

Caroline stopped being grief-stricken and ran to the door of her room.

"News!" Eddie yelped, taking off the baseball cap she wore always and tossing it into the air. "Have I got news!"

Beth stepped out of the bathroom, toothbrush still in her mouth. A year younger than Eddie, ten-year-old Beth had the most beautiful teeth in the Malloy family because she brushed them longer than anyone else. And the reason she brushed them longer was because she always read while she brushed and got so absorbed in her book that she just stood there, going over and over the same teeth for three, four, or even five minutes at a time, her mind on *The Zombie's Revenge* or something.

"Caroline, take off that stupid hat," Eddie said. "We're going camping."

The hat came off with a yank. *"What?"*

"I was in the hardware store buying a wrench for my bike when I heard Mrs. Hatford tell a cus-

4

tomer that her boys were going camping tonight at Smuggler's Cove.''

"Ohhhh!" The very name was delicious. *Smuggler's Cove*. Caroline could almost see people moving about in the moonlight, silent figures carrying sacks off boats and hiding them in caves. The wonderful thing about being an actress, or even *wanting* to be an actress, is that she saw everything as a story, and herself in the starring role.

"But we weren't invited!" said Beth, the toothpaste still foamy around her mouth.

"Of *course* we weren't invited. That's why we're going." Eddie (who was really Edith Ann, but hated her name) picked up her cap from the floor and placed it on her head again, backwards.

"It's a wonderful idea!" cried Caroline. "It's been warm all day. A *perfect* day for camping!"

"We don't even know where Smuggler's Cove is," Beth protested.

"We're going to follow the boys," Eddie said, "only they don't know it. We've got to stay just far enough behind them that they don't see us."

"Then what?" Caroline asked excitedly, her dark eyes shining.

Eddie leaned forward, one arm around Caroline's shoulders, the other around Beth's. *"Then,"* she said, "we steal out in the night and take their clothes."

Both Caroline and Beth shrieked delightedly. Beth was fair-haired and pale-skinned and tended to list to one side in a strong wind. There was no wind here in the upstairs hallway of the house the Malloys were renting, but excitement did the same thing to Beth, and it was only because Eddie had an arm around her that she didn't collapse on the spot.

"They'll have to come back home in their PJs!" Beth cried happily.

"What if they don't wear pajamas?" Caroline asked.

"Then they'll have to come home in their underwear," said Eddie.

"What if they don't sleep in their underwear?" Caroline asked mischievously.

"Then they'll have to walk home stark naked!" said Eddie, and the girls whooped.

·

"We're going camping," Eddie said as the three girls surrounded their mother in the kitchen. "Could we pack our dinner—something to eat cold without cooking?"

Mrs. Malloy looked up from the coupons she was sorting on the table. "Overnight? Where are you going?"

"Smuggler's Cove," Caroline said.

"What?"

"It's a favorite camping spot," Father called from the next room. "I've heard students talk about it on campus."

"Well, I don't know. . . ." said Mother. "I'm not sure—"

"Oh, Jean, don't baby them," Coach Malloy said. "I think it's fine that they want to go camping. Get out in the fresh air and sunshine. Let them go."

Mother sighed. "We don't even have a tent."

"We don't need one! We'll sleep under the stars," Eddie told her. "It's gorgeous out."

So while Mother planned their dinner, the girls ran upstairs for their sleeping bags.

"I heard Mrs. Hatford telling this woman in the hardware store that the boys were going as soon as Jake and Josh finish their paper route this afternoon," Eddie said. "What we've got to do is sit up here with the binoculars. As soon as they start out, we'll follow, just far enough behind that we don't lose them."

Caroline could already see herself as the scout, the spy, Agent XOX, crawling over the desert sand on her stomach, braving the dangers of the night as she slipped one hand under the tent flap and made off with the boys' clothes.

She should really be wearing a cape, she de-

1

cided—a long black cape with a hood that partially covered her face. But there weren't any capes in the Malloy household, so she settled for a large orange poncho that her father wore for college football games when it rained.

She put it on and it dragged the floor. She held it close beneath her chin and watched herself sideways in the mirror as she moved silently around the room.

"Caroline, cut the comedy!" Eddie scolded from the doorway. "The boys could be leaving any minute, and we've got to be ready."

Caroline took off the poncho as Eddie turned on Beth next: "Why are you taking two books? There's not going to be any time to read."

"Just in case," Beth told her. "What do you care, Eddie? I'm the one who's carrying them."

Eddie rolled her eyes and went downstairs to get their dinner.

When Caroline was packed, a sweater, poncho, and pajamas inside her bedroll, she crouched down at her window with Father's binoculars and watched the house across the river with its little balcony on top—a "widow's walk," it was called—supposedly for the wives of sea captains so each could watch for her husband's ship on the horizon. There wasn't any sea near West Virginia,

8

of course—just the shiny horseshoe of a river curving around the end of Island Avenue.

Caroline could make out the two younger boys, Wally and Peter, sitting on the steps, their camping gear behind them, waiting for Jake and Josh to get home. Wally was nine and in the same grade as Caroline. Peter was only seven, and if he hadn't been a Hatford, Caroline thought, she might have liked him because he was sweet and innocent, going along with whatever his brothers thought up because he didn't know any better.

It was Jake and Josh, the eleven-year-old twins, she suspected, who had made the plans about driving the Malloys from Buckman. Jake, especially, who seemed to be the ringleader. But in some ways Josh was worse, because he kept a sketchpad of drawings that made his brothers laugh, and Caroline knew that most of those drawings were cartoons of her and her sisters. When she saw the twins returning with their canvas carriers slung over their shoulders, she gave the signal to Beth, who gave the signal to Eddie, and in minutes the girls were crossing the swinging bridge single file.

They cut through the yard between the Hatfords' place and a neighbor's, careful to stay behind bushes all the way.

Finally they heard the back door slam, and the

four Hatford boys came down the steps, went out the gate at the back of their property, and headed for the woods on the edge of town. Somewhere, in those woods or beyond, was Smuggler's Cove.

Two

•

Smuggler's Cove

It seemed to Wally, sitting on the steps beside Peter, that what he was looking at right now was life. He was studying an anthill built over a crack in the sidewalk. The way the ants were struggling and pushing, each trying to get to the top of the anthill first, reminded him of the way the Hatfords and Malloys had been quarreling since August. As though their quarrel was the most important thing in the world.

"You know what?" he said to Peter. "The ants don't even know we're here. Look." He put his sneakered foot in the path of a large ant hurrying toward the anthill, and it just scurried on around the toe. Didn't even look up to see what giant was blocking its path. Didn't even know that the toe was attached to a foot, and the foot to a leg, and the leg to a body.

"Maybe it's nice to be an ant," he added. "Someone could come along any minute and smash the anthill and they don't even know it. They don't even worry, because it never even crosses their minds."

Peter got up and brought his foot down on the anthill.

Wally stared. "Why did you do *that*?"

"You *said*!"

"I didn't tell you to step on it! You've killed them!"

Peter looked around. "There's more," he said defensively, and sat back down.

Wally sighed. He couldn't help looking up at the sky just then, in case there was the slightest chance of a monstrous foot hanging over him and Peter. He wished that Jake and Josh would hurry and get home from their paper route. On a warm October Saturday like this the battle with the Malloy girls seemed about as important as which ant got to the anthill first. And he, for one, was going to enjoy camping with his brothers—just four guys out in the woods by themselves.

As much as he tried to forget them, however, his mind ran through the inventory of grievances against the girls: the way they had climbed onto the Hatfords' roof one night when Mom and Dad were away and howled through the trapdoor; the way they had spied on the boys from the shed, tricked them into washing the Malloys' windows, and thrown Mom's chocolate chiffon cake in the river.

Wally was smiling in spite of himself. Watching Caroline's face after she'd realized it *was* a cake was the most fun of all. Then he blinked. *Fun?* Did he think *fun?* Was it possible that despite all his grumbling, he *liked* having the girls around?

"What are you grinning about?" asked Peter.

"I was thinking of chocolate cake," Wally told him.

.

"Ham sandwiches, potato salad, Oreo cookies, and apples," said Mother, handing a large bag to Josh as the boys strapped on their gear in the kitchen. "Plus orange drink and doughnuts for breakfast."

"I'll carry the doughnuts," Peter volunteered.

"No, you won't," Jake told him. "The last time you carried the food, you ate all around the edge of two doughnuts. Who's got the water?"

"I have," said Wally.

"Tent?"

"Check," said Josh.

"Flashlight?"

"Check," said Wally.

"I've got the corn chips!" Peter told them.

They were off. Not only did they not have to brush after eating, Wally thought as he went out the back gate with his brothers and headed down the alley, but they could stay up as late as they wanted, and miss Sunday school tomorrow as well.

The bedroll was snug and warm against his back, the leaves thick on the ground, and Wally decided he had never seen such a beautiful October as this one. He could hear the marching band on the college campus, practicing for the homecoming parade the following weekend. Overhead a hawk soared lazily, its wings not even moving. This was a time for eating your supper on a log, lying on your back under the stars, and dreaming about what you were going to be on Halloween.

His left sneaker was sliding up and down on his heel, and Wally looked down to see his shoelace flopping about. He stopped and bent over to tie it, and then his eyes grew large. Staring backwards between his legs he saw, or thought he saw, three figures with packs on their backs who looked all too familiar.

As he stared, however, the three figures seemed to disappear into the trees on either side. Wally stood up and took a deep breath. And then,

. . . .

without even turning around, he caught up with Jake and Josh and Peter.

"Don't anybody look now—don't stop or turn or anything—but we're being followed," he said.

Peter's eyes were like two fried eggs, and his back got as stiff as a broom. "Who is it?"

"Who's the worst you can think of?" Wally said in answer.

"A gorilla?" Peter gulped.

"A motorcycle gang," said Josh. "With chains wrapped around their fists."

But Jake's face registered horror. *Them?* he whispered.

"Them," said Wally. "But don't look. They don't know that we know."

"Who?" Peter demanded.

"Peter, don't you turn around one second. Don't even glance back there, or you're dead meat. Understand?" Jake warned him.

"Who *is* it?" Peter cried. "Robbers?"

"A whomper, a weirdo, and a crazie," Wally answered, reciting the nicknames they'd given Eddie, Beth, and Caroline—Eddie, for the way she could hit a ball; Beth, for the kind of books she read; and Caroline, for turning everything that ever happened to her into a movie.

"Oh, them!" said Peter, obviously relieved. "Are they coming with us?"

"No, they're not coming with us!" croaked Jake.

The boys tramped on, not daring to look around. "Well, I don't know, Jake. I think they're coming whether we want them to or not," Wally said. "They have packs on their backs."

Josh let out his breath. "Somebody must have told them we were going camping. What are we going to do, Jake?"

"Do?" his twin replied. "We are going to make them sorry they tagged along."

"Can I turn around yet?" asked Peter.

"No!" Jake said. "Don't even move your head." And then to Wally, "Think! What would be the worst thing that could happen to them?"

Wally tried to think of the worst thing that had ever happened to *him* in the woods. "Get lost," he said.

Jake's face lit up. "That's *it*! It'll be almost dark in an hour or so. We'll lead the girls every which way until they don't know which end is up. Then we'll sneak down to Smuggler's Cove and have it all to ourselves."

"Wow!" said Peter, his head never moving an inch.

•

It was when they were crossing the creek for the third time that Wally realized they could have been at camp long ago, enjoying their ham sandwiches, if they hadn't felt obliged to lose the girls.

Every so often he or his brothers would slip off into the bushes and wait just long enough to see the girls trailing far behind, and then the boys were off again, hoping to get them royally lost before dark closed in completely.

It was chilly now that the sun was down, and Wally began to wish he had brought his ski cap, as Mom had suggested. Fires were forbidden in the woods in the fall, but once they put up the tent and crawled inside their sleeping bags, they'd be okay.

Wait a minute, he thought. They'd come all the way out here just so he could go to bed at seven o'clock? If he was home he could be watching TV until eleven!

"We've lost them good!" Jake whispered, coming through the bushes behind them. "They're so far back, they'll never catch up. Let's go to the cove and set up camp."

Eager for dinner, the boys hurried through the trees in the direction of the river, and even though Wally's foot slipped once or twice in the mud along the bank, he didn't complain. The last quarter mile or so he turned on the flashlight to see where they were going, and at last they reached the rocky inlet circled by pine trees where the Hatford and Benson boys used to camp summer after summer. Here the river lapped gently against the bank, and the crevasses between the rocks looked deep and forbidding in the near darkness.

"I'll bet old Caroline's bawling her eyes out right now," said Josh.

"How are they going to find their way home?" Peter wanted to know. He was holding the flashlight while his brothers set up the tent. Every so often he tired of holding it still and scanned the trees with it instead, and then all three boys yelled together: "Peter!"

"How are they going to get home?" he asked again.

"That's their problem," said Jake.

"What are they going to eat?" asked Peter, sounding worried.

"That's their problem too," Jake answered. "Did we ask them to follow us out here? Not on your life."

Inside the tent it wasn't so bad. Not so cold, at least. Just crowded. Four boys in one pup tent was two boys too many, but at least it was warmer that way.

Wally didn't think he had ever tasted better ham sandwiches in his life. Thin-sliced ham, with yellow mustard on thick slabs of homemade bread.

Big juicy apples. One carton of potato salad with onion and peppers, and a whole box of Oreo cookies to divide among them, not to mention the doughnuts and orange drink for breakfast.

They all felt much better after they had eaten.

"This is the life!" said Jake, stretching out as best he could on his sleeping bag. "Remember the year the Bensons brought their fishing poles and we had fish for dinner?"

"And the time a mole dug right up into the tent?" said Wally. "And the way Bill Benson used to imitate an owl, and Peter got scared?"

"I did not!" Peter declared. "I knew it was Bill all the time."

"I wonder if they'll ever move back," Wally said, thinking of Bill, Danny, Steve, Tony, and Doug down in Georgia, having a "Georgia peach" for a teacher, and a whole new state to explore. What if their father decided he liked teaching in Atlanta and wanted to stay? What if the Malloys decided they liked being in the Bensons' old house and bought it from them?

It took a lot of fixing and rearranging to get all the sleeping bags squeezed into the pup tent. Everyone complained when Wally took off the sneaker that had got wet and muddy, so he put it back on again, right over his smelly sock.

When they were settled down at last, Wally

turned off the flashlight, and put his hands under his head, staring up into the darkness of the tent. He was wedged between Peter and the left side of the tent, but he was warm at last—and feeling really good with seven Oreo cookies in his stomach.

What did people do who had no brothers? What if he had been born into a family of girls? Three *Malloy* girls! It was a thought too awful to think.

Jake and Josh were trying to make up another verse to "Ninety-nine Bottles of Beer on the Wall," once you got down to "one bottle of beer on the wall," but after a while Jake's voice faded out, then Josh's. Peter had long since fallen asleep, one arm slung over Wally's chest. Finally even Josh stopped singing, and then it was just the sounds of the woods at night—rustling in the bushes, the shrill call of a night bird, the wind blowing through the branches overhead, a deep snore from Josh. . . .

Wally played around with the flashlight awhile, making circles of light on the ceiling of the tent; practiced making distress signals, dots and dashes, with the light. But his eyes began to close, his fingers lost their grip, and finally he tucked the flashlight behind his head and settled down to sleep.

He didn't know when he awakened whether

he had been asleep only a few minutes or an hour, but he felt something moving along his side.

He lay still as a stone. A snake? A *poisonous* snake? Should he move? Should he very, very slowly sit up and wake the others?

Maybe it was another mole. A mouse, perhaps. A harmless little field mouse.

Carefully, carefully, trying not to move his body at all, Wally reached back behind his head for the flashlight. Slowly raising his head so that he could see, he aimed the flashlight toward the moving creature by his side and turned it on.

A hand. A human hand. Wally yelled bloody murder.

Three

•

The Bargain

Caroline was half convinced they would all three die in the woods, and their bodies would not be found until spring. Beth was so tired of going up and down hills and jumping across creeks and climbing over fallen trees that she seemed to be listing to one side rather dangerously. It was also growing dark sooner than they'd thought.

"I think we should all just lie down beside each other with our arms folded over our chests and die peacefully," Caroline said in a hoarse whisper, ever the actress.

"I think you've got rhubarb where your brains should be," Eddie scolded. "Quit whining, you two, and turn on the flashlight."

Beth got out the flashlight. It shone on the path ahead, but the trees still loomed up dark on either side.

"We could all write a farewell note to Mom and Dad, and tell them to give our possessions to the orphans," said Caroline, her voice trembling dramatically.

Eddie wheeled around. "Caroline, will you just shut up? You're not helping things a bit."

"Well, I don't see any point in going any farther when we don't know where we are," Beth said. "We lost the boys a half hour ago, so we might just as well camp here. It's almost dark, and we're starved."

"Listen!" Eddie said suddenly, and the girls stood still.

Caroline listened so hard, she felt her ears were growing, but all she could hear was her own pulse throbbing in her head. And then, far, far away, she thought she heard noises.

"Voices!" Beth confirmed. They listened some more.

"Are you sure they're *human* voices?" Caroline asked. "It could be animal voices. What do raccoons sound like?"

They remained very still and listened again, ears to the wind.

"It almost . . . sounds like singing," Beth said.

They waited.

"It *is* singing," Eddie declared. "It's—"

" 'Ninety-nine Bottles of Beer on the Wall,' " Caroline finished.

"The boys!" the three girls said together.

It took almost fifteen minutes more to get to the place where they could see the tent. First the singing seemed to be coming from one direction. Then the wind changed, and it came from another. Beth got her foot caught in a vine and they had to take her shoe off to get her foot loose. Then it took several more minutes to find the shoe.

By that time the singing had stopped altogether, but Caroline caught sight of a light, a little circle of light, and finally they could hear the river and make out the beam of a flashlight from inside a small tent.

"Bingo!" said Eddie softly. "Okay, let's make camp."

•

Lying on a bed of leaves in the daytime was a lot more pleasant than lying on a bed of leaves in the dark was going to be, with no tent over them, Caroline decided.

As the girls spread out their sleeping bags beneath the trees, Caroline wondered about wild animals.

"Are there bears in West Virginia?" she whispered.

"Cut it out, Caroline," said Eddie.

But Beth gave a little gasp. "Are there?"

"If there are bears in West Virginia, they're way up in the mountains," Eddie said.

Caroline knew that Eddie didn't know what she was talking about any more than Beth knew about bears, but she didn't ask any other questions because she didn't really want to know the answers. She unzipped her sleeping bag, took off her shoes, and crawled in.

"Who's going to steal their clothes?" Beth whispered.

"I am, as soon as I'm sure they're asleep," said Eddie.

Caroline scrunched down as far as she could into her sleeping bag, feeling secure with Eddie on one side of her and Beth on the other. Within minutes Beth began her noisy sleep that sounded like a motorcycle revving up. And then, Caroline could tell from Eddie's slow measured breathing next to her that she had fallen asleep as well.

How could this be? Caroline lay with her eyes wide open. They had come all this way to steal the boys' clothes, and Eddie was asleep? She was just about to poke her and remind her of her obligations, when she remembered the poncho she'd brought along, and Agent XOX. Wasn't it she herself who should be the spy, the scout, the secret agent—creeping through the trees, slithering along the ground, and stealing the boys' clothes?

"Caroline did it again!" her sisters would say in awe.

Wriggling back out of the sleeping bag, she put on her sneakers and picked up the flashlight. Caroline pulled the rubberized poncho over her and then, like a small tepee moving along the ground, set out softly for the boys' tent.

The boys, she figured, would have taken off their clothes and thrown them at the foot of their sleeping bags or perhaps wadded them down between their sleeping bags and the sides of the tent. If she could just slip her hand underneath, perhaps she could pull the clothes out from under the edge without having to open the tent flap at all. Unless, of course, the tent had a canvas floor.

She turned off the flashlight when she reached the tent. Like fingers searching out the keys on a piano, Caroline's fingers inched their way beneath one side. She was in luck. No floor. She lay down on her stomach and extended her arm, her fingers exploring inside the tent.

There was something there, all right. A down jacket? Or was it a sleeping bag she was feeling? She couldn't see a thing, of course, because the poncho had slipped down over her face. Now her hand touched something else and her fingers ran along the edge. Something warm. Somebody's pa-jamas?

"Yipes!" There was a yell from inside the tent.

She tried to pull her hand back, but someone had grabbed it.

Another yell. A bleat. A bellow. "A hand! Josh! Jake!"

Caroline rolled over, struggling hard to pull her arm loose, but someone was pressing it to the ground.

Pushing the poncho off her face, Caroline could see the beam of a flashlight inside the tent, see the jiggling of the canvas as the boys tumbled around, and then the tent flap opened and out they spilled.

"It's Caroline!" yelled Josh. "They found us!"

They found us? They knew? Whoever was inside the tent holding her arm let loose to come outside, and as soon as she was free, Caroline struggled to her feet but tripped on the long poncho and fell on her face again. The boys laughed and yelled.

More footsteps. Running footsteps. Caroline could hear Eddie's voice, trailed by Beth's. Somebody had hold of her feet and was pulling her toward the river. Was Agent XOX to die a drowning death?

"You let go of her!" came Eddie's voice, and suddenly Eddie had one arm, Beth the other, and they were pulling her the other way. Back and forth, back and forth. Secret Agent XOX was going to die a stretching death instead. Torn limb from limb.

"Keep hanging on, and we'll throw you all in!" Jake yelled to Caroline's sisters.

And then Peter's voice wailed sleepily from the door of the tent: "Wally, come back in! It's freezing!"

In that instant Eddie and Beth yanked Caroline free, and finally Caroline was on her feet again, half running, half stumbling back into the underbrush beside her sisters.

•

They sat on top of their sleeping bags while the boys whooped some more and shone the flashlight on them.

"They don't even have a tent!" exclaimed Peter.

"Hey, you girls lost?" Jake's voice.

"You cold? What were you looking for? A blanket?" Wally's.

"You want any directions, just ask us," called Josh. "We'll direct you right into the river."

"Yeah, who asked you to come on this camping trip?" called Jake.

It seemed just too much for Eddie. "You don't

own these woods! You don't own the river! We have as much right to be here as you do!" she screamed.

"Ha! You wouldn't even have found your way out here if you hadn't followed us!" Josh yelled.

"We saw you sneaking along, hiding behind bushes! We knew you were behind us all the time!" called Wally.

Caroline felt her face burning. How embarrassing to know that the boys had known they were back there all the time.

Josh and Jake were laughing again, shining the flashlight right in her eyes. "Old Caroline sneaking over here in that poncho. You look like a witch, Caroline!"

"They're all witches!" declared Josh. "They don't even need to dress up for Halloween. Just come as they are and they'll scare the little kids."

The boys laughed some more.

"Hey, girls!" came Jake's voice. "What are you going to be in the Halloween parade?"

"What Halloween parade?" Caroline called back, in spite of herself. If there was any dressing up in costumes to be done, she wanted to know about it.

"The school parade," yelled Wally. "We and the Bensons won first prize almost every year."

"Well, whatever we think of, it'll be a lot better than what *you* wear," Beth retorted.

"You wish!" said Josh.

"We'll win again, won't we, Wally?" came Peter's voice.

"Sure we will."

"Wanna bet?" yelled Eddie. "You must feel you own this town. You must think you're going to go on winning the prizes and hogging the best camping spots just because you lived here first. Well, I'll tell you something, wise guys. Maybe you *won't*! Maybe somebody else will win this year."

"Keep dreaming!" called Josh.

Caroline was beginning to shiver. The air seemed cooler than it had when she'd started out for the boys' tent, and she wished Beth and Eddie would crawl into their sleeping bags and shut up. But Eddie was angry, and when she was angry, she was unstoppable.

"Wanna bet?" she yelled again.

"Sure! Bet!" yelled Jake. "Whichever group wins first prize—you or us—will be the masters and the other group will be the slaves."

Were they crazy? Caroline wondered. *No one would agree to—*

"You're on!" Eddie yelled back. "Deal!"

Caroline gasped. "Eddie, are you nuts?"

"They think they're *so* smart!" Eddie sputtered. Caroline had never seen her so angry.

"What will the slaves have to do?" Caroline called out.

Josh answered, "Whatever the masters tell them to do."

There seemed to be a brief discussion going on in the boys' camp. Then Wally replied, "The slaves have to do all the masters' work for a whole month."

"Fine with us!" yelled Eddie.

"Eddie, if they win, they'll—" Beth began.

"They *won't*! *We* will!" Eddie said. And then, more desperately, "We *have* to!"

Caroline let out her breath. She was too tired to argue anymore. All she wanted was her warm sleeping bag and a soft place to lay her head. She had just started to crawl in when suddenly, *Splat*.

Caroline looked around. Another splat.

"Rain!" cried Beth and Eddie together.

The girls quickly rolled up their cotton sleeping bags, sat on top of them, and spread out the poncho over their heads, while the boys whooped again and tumbled back into their tent.

The rain came down harder and harder. Fifteen minutes. Twenty minutes. On and on. All around them the ground was getting soggy and spongy. A damp earth smell arose from the floor of the forest. Caroline felt like a mushroom. She smelled like a mushroom. She imagined that she had little bugs crawling up one side of her stalk and down the other.

The food was gone. The water was almost gone. Caroline needed to go to the bathroom, but she didn't want to get rained on, so she stayed where she was and felt miserable.

It was all such a dumb idea, following the boys out here to steal their clothes. They hadn't even taken their clothes off, come to think of it, and neither had she or her sisters.

"Hey, girls!" came a yell from down on the riverbank. "You going to stay there and get wet?"

"Why don't you find your way home?"

"Are your sleeping bags soggy?"

Caroline could hear her teeth chattering. Or maybe it was Eddie's or Beth's. For a while none of them moved. None of them spoke. The rain drummed on the poncho over their heads, and Caroline was sure that by morning it would have driven them all mad. None of them spoke; they were too disgusted and angry.

And then, after a long while, Eddie murmured, "Wait till Halloween!" And she said it with conviction.

Four

•

Spy

All the way home from Smuggler's Cove, Wally worried.

First, he worried that the girls might not have found their way home. When he and his brothers went looking for them the next morning, all they had found was a sock.

Second, he worried that if they *did* make it home all right, Caroline and her sisters really might win first prize in the Halloween parade, and he and his brothers would have to do the girls' work for a month. He tried to imagine going over to the Malloys' house for four Saturdays asking Caroline what needed doing. Imagined her telling him to make her bed and wash her clothes. Maybe even clean the toilets!

Josh must have been thinking the same thing. "Jake," he said as they turned up the alley behind their house, "maybe we should pull out of that bargain with the Malloys. What if we *don't* win?"

"We will!" Jake said. "Don't even talk about not winning! What we've got to do now is think up the best costumes we've ever had."

Wally wondered what it would be like to live on Mars. He imagined that he might see a note on the school bulletin board Monday that said, *Wanted: Boys to live on Mars for one month. Girls need not apply.* He would go. He would be first in line. He would come back to earth just as the horrible month of being slaves to the Malloys was up.

He tried to think of a costume to end all costumes. He remembered how the Hatfords and Bensons had once painted black stripes on their white T-shirts, chained themselves together, and walked in the parade as a chain gang. Another time they had all worn cardboard fronts and backs, painted black with white dots, and entered the contest as a set of dominoes. They had even been a fly swatter and bugs. Wally didn't see how the girls could ever come up with something better than that. They might, though. The only thing the boys could think of to do this Halloween was to go as "punkin' heads," with pumpkins cut out at the bottom so that Wally and his brothers could slip their heads up inside from underneath.

"What we need to do," he said, almost to himself, "is spy on the girls and see what they're going to be. Just in case."

"I was thinking the same thing," said Josh, busily making a sketch of Caroline in the poncho, almost being tossed into the river. Josh took a sketchpad wherever he went. "One of us has to be a mole."

"A mole?" asked Wally.

"A spy from the inside out," said Jake, and they all turned toward Peter.

"What's the matter?" Peter asked warily. "Why are you looking at *me*?"

"How would you like to be a mole?" said Jake.

"The most important job you've ever had," added Josh.

"And if you goof up, we're dead meat," said Wally. He heard Peter swallow.

•

At school the next day there was not a notice on the bulletin board requesting boys to go to Mars. There was a sign-up sheet outside the principal's office for entering the Halloween contest. Some students wanted to be in the parade just for the fun of dressing up, but others wanted to be judged on their costumes. If you wanted to be judged, you were supposed to put your name on the sign-up sheet and say whether you were coming as a group or as an individual.

Jake saw the sign-up sheet first, and right there at the top, under group entry, he wrote: *The Hatfords: Jake, Josh, Wally, and Peter.*

By lunchtime there was another entry on the sheet under "group": *The Malloys—Eddie, Beth, and Caroline.*

It was official. This time *Wally* swallowed.

"Think!" said Jake when the boys got home. "What excuse can we think of to send Peter over there to look around?"

"Maybe he could ask Caroline about your homework assignment, Wally," said Josh.

"Are you nuts?" said Wally. "She's the last person I'd ask, and she knows it."

"Peter could ask to borrow a cup of sugar," said Jake.

Josh wrinkled his nose. "That's about the phoniest excuse there is."

Everybody looked at Wally.

"He could return Caroline's sock," Wally said.

"Bingo!" said Jake and Josh together.

They sat Peter on the kitchen table, gave him half a Hershey bar that Jake had been carrying around in his pocket, and went over his instructions.

"Here's what you do," said Jake. "You go up to

the Malloys' front door and ask for Caroline. When she comes to the door, give her the sock and tell her you were worried about whether she got home okay."

"I was?" asked Peter.

"Well . . . sure. I mean, we were all wondering . . . uh . . . sort of . . . whether the girls got home all right in the rain," said Jake. "We didn't want them to get wet, did we?"

"You were ready to throw her in the *river*!" Peter said.

"Oh, not really. Just trying to scare her a little," Josh told him.

"She'll probably make some nasty remark, but just ignore her. Keep saying you were worried, and here's her sock, and then ask if they could give you any ideas of what you could be in the Halloween parade," Jake told him.

"No, I've got it!" said Josh. "Tell them we won't let you be in the parade with us, and you want to be in the parade with them. They probably won't let you, but if you pay attention, they'll probably give some clue about what their costume is going to be."

Peter's face clouded up and Wally began to feel very uncomfortable.

"But I *can* be in the parade with you, can't I?"

"Sure, but you're just saying that so—"

"Then it's a lie," Peter said flatly.

"No, it's not, Peter, because right now I'm telling you that you can't be in the parade with us, but after you come back from the Malloys, I'll tell you that you can."

"But—"

"Just *do* it, Peter! Just take Caroline's sock and see what you can find out."

"I always have to do everything!" Peter grumbled, yanking the sock out of Jake's hand, sliding off the table, and banging out the door.

Jake and Josh and Wally looked at each other.

"What do you bet he doesn't do it?" said Jake.

"He'll probably just drop the sock in the river and say he couldn't find out anything," said Josh.

"I'm going to follow along behind him just in case," Wally said, moving over to the window. He waited until Peter had got as far as the swinging bridge, then slipped out the door himself.

Since the Malloys had come to Buckman, nothing was the same, Wally thought, hands in his jacket pockets. He and his brothers couldn't even enjoy Halloween without worrying what the girls would wear in the parade. Just when he thought maybe they could forget the girls for a change, he had to worry what it would be like to lose the contest to Eddie, Beth, and Caroline and have them boss him around for a whole month. That was about the stupidest bargain Jake had ever made. It was dumber than dumb.

Up ahead, Peter was in no particular hurry to get to the Malloys'. He was placing the heel of one foot against the toe of the other, and he must have been counting with every step, because every so often he slapped the sock against the cable hand-rail and said, "Ten!" More steps. "Twenty! . . ."

Wally waited until his younger brother was across the bridge and had disappeared behind the trees on the other side before he went across himself. He quickened his steps as he reached the end because he wanted to make sure he was there in the bushes when Peter knocked on the door.

When Wally stepped off the end of the bridge, however, he paused, with one foot in the air, because Peter was not five yards away from him, stooping to fill Caroline's sock with stones.

Wally let out his breath. At this rate Peter would reach the Malloy house about midnight! He started to say something, then realized Peter prob-ably wouldn't go up to the house at all if he knew Wally was watching, so he stood motionless, wait-ing, until Peter stood up and trudged on again, holding the bulging sock in one hand and whirling it around and around above his head.

When he came to the picket fence next to the Malloys', Peter dragged the sock along it . . .

whumpity, whumpity, whump . . . and began singing at the same time: "This old man, he played one, *he* played *knick*knack *on* my *thumb* . . ." And when he reached the end of the Malloys' driveway, Peter stopped and sang the next verse of the song holding his nose: "This old man, he played two, he played knickknack on my shoe . . ." When that was done, he pulled his bottom lip out away from his teeth and sang the third verse like that.

Wally didn't think he could stand it. He wondered if he should go grab the sock and try to find out something from Caroline himself, but he knew it would never work. Caroline would never, ever give him even the slightest clue about what the girls were going to be on Halloween. There was nothing to be done but wait it out.

At long last Peter sighed, straightened, dumped the stones out of the sock, and finally went up the driveway to the Malloys' front porch.

Wally crept along in the bushes by the side of the driveway, and finally made it up to the garage. He peeked around the corner.

Knock, knock, knock.

At first it didn't seem as though anyone was home. No one came to the door, and Peter even went over to a window and peeped in. He turned and started back down the steps. Wally wanted to yell, *Not yet! Try again!* when the door behind Peter opened.

"What do *you* want?"

Crazy Caroline herself!

"Uh . . . I—I . . ." Peter stammered.

"Well?"

Peter held out the sock. "I was worried about you," he said.

Good job! Wally thought. *Nice going, Peter!*

The irritation on Caroline's face gave way to surprise. "Why?"

"If you got home okay."

"Why were you worried about me when you were trying to throw me in the river? You weren't very worried then."

"I wasn't trying to throw you in the river. I was asleep in the tent," Peter told her.

Caroline's face softened immediately, and Wally wondered whether girls always felt motherly toward smaller children. Sisterly, anyway.

"Well, maybe you *were* in the tent. I couldn't see."

"All that was left of you was this sock," Peter went on in a small voice. Wally decided that if their family ever became poor, they could send Peter out to beg on street corners, because he obviously could wring your heart.

"Who is it, Caroline?" came a voice from in-side.

"Peter Hatford. He found my sock."

"What?" Eddie stuck her head out the door, then came out on the porch, followed by Beth.

"He says he was worried about me. He was in the tent when his goon brothers tried to throw me in the river."

"They weren't really," Peter said. "They were only fooling."

"Now you tell me," said Caroline.

"But I was worried you might not find your way home in the rain," Peter plowed on.

Eddie studied him quizzically. "My, aren't we concerned all of a sudden," she said.

"I'm sure Josh and Jake and Wally were awake all night worrying about us," said Beth. "Nobody came over and offered to let us share your tent, though. If you ask me, Peter, I think you've got three baboons for brothers."

Wally strained to hear what they were saying next, but from where he stood behind the garage, he didn't think they were saying anything at all. Looking around the corner, it seemed to Wally as though the girls were whispering among them-selves.

And suddenly he heard Eddie saying, "It was really nice of you to bring back Caroline's sock,

Peter. You want to come in for some peanut butter cookies?"

No, Peter, no! Wally thought desperately. *It's a trap! Don't do it! Don't go!*

But even as he thought it, he saw Peter's head bob up and down, and a moment later Peter disappeared into the Malloys' house, followed by Eddie, Beth, and Caroline, all three of them grinning.

Five

•

A Little Chat with Peter

It was the chance of a lifetime, and Caroline and her sisters knew it. Mother was at the dentist's, and they had Peter all to themselves. He was as gullible as a dry sponge; he'd soak up whatever they told him, but one squeeze, and he'd probably leak out all the Hatfords' secrets.

Beth and Eddie were thinking the same thing, because Peter had scarcely sat down at the kitchen table before there was an orange soda and a plate of cookies in front of him, with a little package of M&M's on the side.

"Tell me, Peter," said Eddie, "do your brothers *always* act like goons, or is it just around us?"

"Well, sometimes . . . I mean . . ." Peter seemed to be thinking it over, his mouth full of cookies. "Well, most of the time they're . . . Well, you know what? They won't even let me be in the Halloween parade with them, and I wanted to know if I could be in it with you."

Caroline knew a trap when she heard it. She could see it, smell it, and so could Beth and Eddie. The three girls exchanged looks. Actually, they had just that morning discussed the matter of a group costume, and decided to go as a centipede—three legs and three arms sticking out one side, three legs and three arms sticking out the other. Four arms and four legs would be even better, but how did they know Peter was telling the truth?

"Well, I don't know," said Beth. "We were planning to go as gypsies. Isn't that right, Eddie? I'm not sure you'd make such a good gypsy, Peter."

"Oh, yeah. Gypsies. Right!" said Caroline. "Sure you want to dress up in bracelets and stuff, Peter?"

"Huh-uh," said Peter, and took a long drink of orange soda.

Caroline sat down on one side of him. "Why won't your brothers let you be in the parade with them?"

"I don't know," Peter told her, and opened the package of M&M's.

Beth sat down on the other side. "I would think that *four* boys would have a better chance of winning the prize than three."

No answer.

Eddie tried next. "It's easy to think up a costume if you're a boy. All boys have to do is put on old clothes and be bums or something. They hardly have to do any work."

"Uh-*uh*!" said Peter. "We've got to cut holes in the bottoms of pumpkins for our heads to go through and—" He stopped, looking suddenly confused. Caroline and Eddie exchanged triumphant glances.

"Oh, I forgot!" cried Peter. "That was last year! Yeah, that's what we were *last* year. Punkin' heads. *This* year we're going as pirates. Yeah, *pirates*! I *forgot*!"

"Sure, Peter. Right. Pirates are a swell costume. I'll bet that'll win first prize," smiled Beth.

Looking much relieved, Peter grinned back and took another long drink of soda.

He was so cute that Caroline almost wished he were *her* little brother. At the same time it seemed foolish not to get all the information out of him that they could.

"Peter," she said, trying to sound as motherly as possible—if she were to become an actress, she would undoubtedly be asked, at some time in her life, to play the part of a mother—"tell me something; why do your brothers hate us?"

"They don't *hate* you," said Peter uncertainly. "They just don't like you very much."

"Oh, that makes me feel so much better!" said Beth.

"I mean, well, they *like* you, sort of, but . . . you're not boys!"

"How stupid of us!" said Eddie. "We're so sorry."

Peter plowed on. "It's just that we liked the Bensons better."

"Can *we* help it if the Bensons moved away?" Caroline asked. "Why take it out on us?"

Peter thought that one over too. "Well . . . see . . . if *you* go back to Ohio, and the Bensons can't find anybody to rent their house to, then maybe they'll come back."

"I get it," said Caroline. "Your baboon brothers think that if they make us miserable enough, we'll leave."

Peter nodded. "But *I* don't want you to be miserable."

"Of course not," said Eddie.

"You just want us to leave too," said Beth.

Peter reached for another cookie. "Well, not *exactly*, because . . . Wally doesn't want you to leave either."

Caroline was genuinely surprised. "He *doesn't*?"

"No. I mean, not yet. He said he wants you to stay in Buckman until we've done all the things we wanted to do to you and then . . . I mean . . . well . . ."

"Oh, we understand perfectly," said Beth.

Caroline sighed dramatically. "I guess we just can't win. No matter what we do, the boys will always get the best of us."

"Right," said Beth. "Pirates will always win a costume contest before gypsies. But I can't think of anything else to be, can you, Caroline?"

As Beth put the cookies back in the pantry, however, Caroline followed her in.

"Listen, Beth, are you *sure* we shouldn't try to get Peter to be in our costume with us? *Four* arms and legs would make an even better centipede, and he could be the tail."

"No. He'll give it away. Somehow he'd leak it to the others."

"Yes, but think how great it would be if we win first place and Peter was on our side! Like we'd recruited him right out from under their noses."

"Better to keep him as spy and not even let on that he is. No telling when we'll need him again," said Beth.

They went back in the kitchen where Peter was finishing his drink, and when he put his glass down

he had a wide orange mustache above his upper
lip.

"Thanks for bringing back my sock, Peter.
Come over anytime," Caroline told him.

"Okay," Peter said, and after he went outside,
he shuffled down the driveway, stopping to pick up
an acorn, then another and another, filling his
pockets with them, and skipping on.

"Too bad he's a Hatford," said Beth, watching.

But Eddie disagreed. "It's *great* he's a Hatford.
Don't you realize what a coup this is! A spy in their
own camp! I'm *sure* those guys are going as punkin' heads. They sent Peter over here to make us
believe they were going as pirates, and he let the
cat out of the bag. This is more fun than I thought."

"You know what's going to happen, though,
don't you? They'll win!" said Beth. "Four guys
with pumpkins on their heads will win over a centipede any day."

A glum silence settled down over the room.

"Then there's only one thing to do," said Eddie. "We've got to go over there before the parade
and smash those pumpkins to bits."

"Eddie!"

Both Caroline and Beth looked shocked.

"That's playing dirty," said Beth.

"And they weren't? Sending Peter over here to
try and find out what we were going to be on Hal-

loween? And Peter's story about their being pirates? That was the lowest thing they could do."

"Still . . ."

"Still nothing! I'll smash their pumpkins myself."

"What if they keep the pumpkins in their house?"

"I doubt it. Once you carve a pumpkin it starts to stink if you keep it inside."

"We'd better make that centipede costume extra good just in case," said Caroline.

In a way, Caroline wished that they were going as something other than a bug. A centipede was okay, but she wished it could be something a bit more dramatic. An aspiring actress, she knew, was constantly on the lookout for life experiences that enabled her to practice a role, and she did not know of any plays or movies that would require her to play the part of a centipede. Still, if she were the *head* of the centipede instead of the tail . . .

"Could I be the head?" she asked her sisters. "I mean, maybe we could tell a little story. Maybe the head of the centipede always wants to go one way but the tail wants to go another. Or maybe the head of the centipede could be crying, and—"

Eddie sighed. "Caroline, for gosh sake, do you have to turn everything into a catastrophe? Can't you just be a *bug* for once and—"

"Well, maybe she has a point," said Beth. "It's got to be a pretty unusual centipede to win first prize."

Back in Ohio their school did not have contests. There was a Halloween party every year, but no parade around the business district, and no prizes for best costume. Caroline had dreaded moving to West Virginia because she thought it would be all mountains and cabins and coal mines, and here was a town with a college and a river and a swinging bridge and, best of all, an elementary school with an auditorium and stage.

An auditorium with a stage and a thick velvet curtain—gold on one side, maroon on the other. Caroline knew, she was utterly convinced, that someday she would perform on that stage, and it wouldn't be as a centipede either.

The door opened and Mother came in. She looked the same, but sounded different. And when she poured a glass of water and tried to drink, water trickled out one side of her mouth.

"Novocaine," she said, with a laugh. "I can't feel a thing." She looked around the kitchen at the empty glass and the cookie crumbs on a plate. "Looks like you've had a party."

"A little welcoming party," said Beth dryly.

"For whom?"

"Peter Hatford was by to pay us a visit," said Caroline.

"One of the Hatford boys? How nice! You know, I think our two families got off on the wrong foot somehow," Mother told them. "One of these days I'm going to bake them a pie to thank those boys for washing our windows. I think that would be a friendly gesture, don't you?"

Caroline, Beth, and Eddie exchanged looks.

"Maybe," said Caroline. "Maybe not."

Six

•

Birds of Prey

Peter had just stepped off the end of the bridge when three sets of hands grabbed him and he let out a squeal.

"What happened?" asked Wally. "What happened after you got inside?"

Peter licked at the rim of orange soda around his mouth. "We had a party," he said grandly, and kept walking.

Jake and Josh moaned.

"What *happened*?" Wally asked again.

"Well," said Peter, crossing the road, the boys keeping step beside him, "first we sat down in the kitchen, and Eddie poured me some orange soda, and then Beth got out the cookies, and—"

"Never mind the *food*, Peter, what *happened*?" Wally was beside himself.

"Let me *tell* it, Wally! And then Caroline gave me some M&M's and—"

"Those were bribes, Peter. Couldn't you tell?"

"They were *good*!" Peter went up on the porch. "And then Caroline asked why we hated them."

"She did? Caroline thinks we *hate* them?"

"And I said we didn't hate them, we just wanted them to stay long enough for us to do all the stuff we wanted to do to them and—"

Jake sank down on the steps. "We're dead," he said.

"We should never have let Peter go by himself," agreed Josh.

"Peter," said Wally, trying his best to be patient, "tell me the truth. Did you tell them we were going to be punkin' heads in the parade?"

"No! I told them that's what we were *last* year."

Jake and Josh groaned again.

"I told them that *this* year we were going to be pirates."

"But did you find out what *they* are going to be?" Wally asked.

This time Peter actually beamed. "I found out a secret!"

"What?" cried his three brothers at once.

"Well, *they* said they were going to be gypsies in the parade."

"Gypsies? They told you that?"

"That's what they said, but when Caroline and Beth went in the pantry, I heard them talking, and Caroline said they were going to be . . ." Peter's face blanched suddenly. "I—I forgot!"

This time Jake dramatically tumbled down the steps and lay stretched out on the sidewalk below. "I can't stand it."

Wally grabbed Peter by the shoulders. "Peter, a whole month depends on this—who's going to be boss, them or us."

"Um . . ." said Peter thoughtfully.

"What letter did it begin with? Can you even remember that?" pleaded Jake.

"S," said Peter.

"Scarecrows?" guessed Jake.

"No."

"A salad bowl—carrots and onions and stuff?" guessed Wally.

"Not something to eat." Peter frowned.

"Sheep?" asked Jake. "Sheep and shepherd?"

"No. Not an animal."

Wally was desperate. He would rather jump off the bridge than be the Malloys' slave for a month. He tried to think of everything he knew that began with an *s:* "Soap, sewing basket, spit, sandwich, shoes, stockings, snakes, soccer, slugs, slime . . ."

Peter's face lit up suddenly: "I know! It crawls!"

"Okay," Jake said excitedly. "We're getting close. It crawls, but it's not an animal."

"No. It's a—a bug. I think."

"Spider!" shouted Wally.

"No . . . it's got a lot of legs," Peter told them.

"A centipede?" Wally asked.

"Yes! That's it! A centipede!" Peter cried delightedly.

"That begins with a *c*, dope," said Jake.

"Never mind, we got it! A centipede, huh?" said Josh. "Oh, boy, how are we going to top that?"

"Think, Wally!" Jake said, as he always did when they needed an idea. "What could top a centipede? You know how the principal's always saying we should act the part—witches should act spooky and scarecrows should walk stiff-legged and soldiers should march and everything? What could mess up a centipede just by acting its part?"

Everyone looked at Wally.

"A giant boot," said Wally.

It was a good idea except that no one knew how four boys could be a giant boot, and even if they were, how could it come down on top of the girls, and even if it did, what was the good of that when they'd be expelled from the parade, not to mention school?

"Think some more," said Jake.

"A fly swatter," said Wally.

That had the same problems as a giant boot.

Wally tried to put his mind in the Destructo Mode. *Stamp, swat, squash, smash, swallow* . . .

Swallow!

"What eats insects?" he said aloud. "Birds. We could be birds."

"Birds?" asked Jake, not at all sure. "Who wants to be in a Halloween parade dressed as sparrows or something?"

"Not sparrows," said Wally, and suddenly he began to smile. "What about some big, horrible repulsive bird? What about vultures?"

"That's *it*!" cried Jake. "We're a flock of vultures! And right in the middle of the parade we'll descend on the centipede and tear its skin off."

Peter looked alarmed.

"Oh, we're not going to hurt anyone," said Jake. "All we'll do is play the part of a vulture and pull off the girls' costume. If anyone bawls us out, we'll say we were acting the part."

Peter's chin trembled a little. "They gave me cookies," he said.

Wally sat down beside him. "Listen, Peter, would you like it if every time you were on a swing at school, Caroline told you to get off so she could have it?"

"N-no."

"What if Eddie made you come over and clean her room? Or do their dishes? Don't you see what would happen if the girls win first prize and we have to be their slaves?"

"I guess."

"That's why we've got to be vultures," Jake told him. "Wally, find out everything you can about vultures."

•

The library was open on Monday nights, so after dinner Wally rode his bike over to the corner of East Main Street and Sedgwick. He looked up *vulture* in the encyclopedia. It didn't tell him much he didn't already know.

"Try our new *Birds of Prey* book," the librarian suggested, and pointed to a shelf under the window.

Wally found the book and sat down with his paper and pencil. He started reading and his eyes grew wide. He read some more and his mouth fell open. He could not believe what was there on the page.

A half hour later he was on his way home again, pedaling as fast as he could. Mom and Dad were out in the garden by the side of the house, picking the last of the tomatoes before they were killed by frost. Peter was on the living-room floor, building something with his Lego set, and Jake and Josh had their books spread out on the dining room table, doing their math assignment, when Wally burst through the front door.

"You are absolutely not going to *believe* this!" he told them. Peter got up and came over.

"Did you find out a lot of stuff we could do in the parade? Vulture stuff?" asked Jake.

"Hoo boy!" said Wally. He unfolded the piece of paper he had scribbled on at the library. "Number one," he read. "Vultures can soar as high as 26,000 feet."

"I'll do that one," Jake joked.

"They have a six-foot wingspan."

"Get real," said Josh.

"They eat road kill," Wally went on.

"That's you, Josh," said Jake.

"But their favorite food is rotting fish guts."

"That's you, Jake," said Josh.

"When they're scared, they throw up."

"That's you, Wally," laughed Jake and Josh together.

"And they cool themselves by peeing on their legs."

"That's Peter!" they all said at once.

"That's *not*! I won't do it! You always try to make me do everything!" Peter bellowed.

"But that's not the worst," Wally told them. "When the vulture is *really* upset, it . . . well, doo-doos. *Vigorously.*"

"How are we supposed to do all that in the Halloween parade?" asked Jake.

"Well, I don't know, but here's what we'd look like," said Josh, turning his paper over. "Maybe if we made some beaks out of papier-mâché, and some feet with claws . . ."

He immediately set to work.

·

At school the next day Wally was very, very careful not to act as though he knew that the Malloy girls were going to be a centipede. He was very, very careful not to even say the word *centipede*. Even when Caroline Malloy, who sat behind him, got restless in geography as she usually did and began bumping the back of his chair with her knees, he didn't even turn around.

When school was out that afternoon, he sat on the steps in the crisp October sunshine, collar turned up around his neck, and waited for Jake and Josh to come out. He was watching one lone leaf as it dangled from a branch above, twisting this way and that in the wind, and Wally wondered what it was like to be a leaf. Did it stay on the tree until its stem was dry and withered, then drop, or did it just suddenly think to itself one day, *That's it; I'm tossing in the towel,* or did it—

Suddenly the door banged again and out came Josh, his head down, Jake close at his heels.

"Gosh *darn* it!" Josh yelped, throwing his jacket on the ground. Then he picked it up and threw it again.

"What's wrong?" asked Wally.

"We had to trade papers for math and grade each other's," Jake explained.

"So?"

"So Josh had to trade with Eddie."

"So?" Wally said again.

"Eddie found the picture of the vulture that Josh drew on the back of his math paper," Jake told him.

Seven

•

Change of Plans

"You won't *believe* this!"

Eddie was waiting when Caroline and Beth came out of the building at three o'clock. The Hatford boys were already far down the sidewalk, their shoulders hunched against the wind.

"What?" cried Caroline.

"You won't *believe* it!" Eddie said again. "If you ever thought the Hatford boys might really be nice underneath, or kind, or polite, think again."

"What did they *do*?" insisted Beth.

"It's not what they did, it's what they were planning to do."

"*What?*" Caroline shouted. "Tell us!"

"I can't. Some things just have to be shown."

When they walked in the house, they all said hi to Mother, who was making a corn husk wreath to go on the front door, and went straight up to Eddie's room, which looked like the locker room of the New York Mets, because there were baseball pictures everywhere.

"Look." Eddie threw her books on the bed and sat down. Then, reaching into her jacket pocket, she pulled out a folded piece of paper. "I was supposed to give this back to Josh after I graded it, but I didn't."

Caroline leaned over and stared at the paper. "It says, *Math, 4 wrong.*"

Eddie turned the paper over. Caroline looked again. In the center of the picture was a drawing of a small centipede. There were three legs and three arms sticking out one side of it, three legs and three arms sticking out the other. And hovering over the centipede were four large ferocious-looking vultures, who were holding it down with their claws.

"They know!" Beth gasped.

"More than that," said Eddie. "*They're* going as vultures! Or *were*. But read the fine print."

Caroline looked hard at the first vulture.

Jake, it said above the vulture's head, and then, printed along the side: *Eats rotten fish guts. Josh*, it said above the second vulture: *Throws up on the centipede.*

"Gross!" cried Beth.

"It gets worse," said Eddie.

"Wally," read Caroline aloud, pointing to the third vulture. She studied the dotted line from the vulture to the centipede, then turned the paper sideways to see what this vulture was doing. *"Pees on the centipede!"* She stared aghast, but Beth snatched the paper away.

"Peter," she read. "Peter . . . doo—" She gasped. "Peter does the doo-doo."

"They wouldn't!" cried Caroline.

"I don't know what they'd do, but I never met four more disgusting guys in my life," said Eddie.

They sat motionless on the bed, staring at each other.

"So much for the centipede," said Beth.

"I wouldn't be a centipede for anything in the world," said Caroline.

"Then *think*!" said Eddie. "What *are* we going to be in the parade? We've got to be a bunch of something."

"Bananas?" said Caroline.

"It's been done."

"M&M's?"

"Everybody does that. Last year there were two groups of M&M's at our school back home. It's not original enough."

"One of us could be the Energizer rabbit, and the other two could be batteries," said Caroline.

Eddie sighed in disgust.

"How about if I go as a tube of Cheez Whiz, and you two go as crackers?"

"Thanks a lot," said Beth.

"Two dogs and a fire hydrant?" suggested Caroline, amazed at her own creativity.

"Not bad," said Eddie.

"A parking meter and two coins?"

"Keep going."

They thought of a toothbrush and molars, or Oxy pads and zits, but when they thought about how to make the costumes it just got too complicated.

"The point is," said Eddie, "the principal will be the judge. What *we* might like, and what the principal might like, are two different things entirely. It should probably be something with a lesson to it."

"Ugh." Caroline clutched her throat.

"I know, I know, but we've *got* to win first prize, Caroline. Do you want to be the Hatfords' slaves? Think what will happen if we lose! Do we really want to wash their socks and clean their bathtub and take out their trash every week?"

It was a distressing thought.

"What does the principal like?" asked Caroline.

"Trees," said Beth. "He really likes trees.

Somebody told me that every spring, he plants a tree at the end of the school yard."

"And did you ever read the poem he has framed above his bookcase? 'I think that I shall never see, a poem lovely as a tree . . .' " said Caroline dramatically.

"Okay," said Eddie. "We'll go as a shrub, with sticks taped to our arms for branches. Each of us will be a limb—a large limb. We'll be bound together at the waist and knees, so our legs form a thick trunk, but we'll each sort of spread our arms and wave them slowly in the wind. The principal will love it."

•

When Caroline woke the next morning, she had no idea that this would be one of the most wonderful days of her life, and it had nothing to do with a shrub.

"And now, class," the teacher said after she took the roll, "for those of you who are new at Buckman this year, we have a tradition you may not know about. Every spring the sixth grade puts on a play for the rest of the school"—Carolyn's heart sank. Only the *sixth* grade?—"but every October the fourth grade puts on a Halloween play for the lower grades."

Joy in the morning!

"It's not a very long play, because small children can't sit still very long, so there won't be a lot to memorize, but I think you'll find it fun."

Carolyn felt as though she were floating above the desks.

"This year I have selected *The Goblin Queen* for our play. As I read each part, if you think you would be interested, please raise your hand. First, the queen herself—"

Caroline's hand was in the air before the words had even left the teacher's mouth.

"Caroline?" said the teacher. "Is that all?"

Two more hands went up.

"Caroline, Nancy, and Kim," the teacher said. "You'll try out at lunchtime, girls, and we'll see who reads it best."

Caroline *was* floating. *She* could read it best. She knew she could.

"Three witches . . ." the teacher went on.

More hands went up, and the teacher wrote more names on the board.

"A grandfatherly ghost . . . a black cat . . . two skeletons . . ." The list went on and on, and more names were added. Wally didn't volunteer for a thing, Caroline noticed, but she didn't care.

After lunch she sat in a little circle by the teacher's desk, and one by one she and Nancy and Kim read the lines that the Goblin Queen would say. Caroline wonderfully, gloriously, deliriously outdid the other girls. Even Nancy and Kim had to admit it. "Caroline did it best," they said.

"Well, you two girls will be her goblins-in-waiting, then," Miss Applebaum said, "and those are good parts too. You are all good readers."

"Will the play be in the auditorium?" Caroline asked breathlessly. "Up on stage . . . with the velvet curtain and everything?"

The teacher looked amused. "Yes, Caroline, at long last, it will be up on stage in the auditorium with the velvet curtain and everything. The seats won't be filled, of course, only the first few rows, but it will be an appreciative audience. Everyone looks forward to the Halloween play."

•

When Caroline walked out of school that day, she came down the steps slowly, her back straight, head high, as a queen would walk as she stepped off the throne to greet her subjects.

"What's the matter, Caroline, a crick in your neck?" asked Eddie.

"You," said Caroline, "are looking at the actress with the leading role in the fourth-grade play, *The Goblin Queen.*"

"Gobble the Queen?" teased Beth.

Caroline gave her a haughty glance.

"I was the very best one in tryouts, and I will perform onstage!" And then she couldn't contain herself. She grabbed her sisters by the arms and dissolved in happy giggles. "Oh, Eddie! Beth! I'm so excited. We really get to be onstage, with the curtain and everything!"

"Well, just don't let it go to your head, Caroline," Eddie told her. "We've still got our costume to be working on, because if we don't win that contest, *Wally's* going to be king and you're going to be his loyal subject. And if that's not enough to make you throw up, I don't know what is."

Caroline sighed. "Ugh. What should we be doing?"

"We should be finding sticks to tape to our arms. Not too heavy, though, or our arms will get tired."

When the girls got across the swinging bridge, they went down the bank on the other side, where there were low-hanging branches, and looked for sticks that had fallen on the ground.

"I've got two, with lots of twigs on them," said Caroline, holding them up in the air. "How do these look, Eddie?"

Beth held hers up, too, to see if they would be too heavy.

"Do we look like a tree?" she asked.

"A good-sized shrub, maybe," said Eddie. She

stood on tiptoe to break off a long branch that was already dangling and added it to the others. "I think this will do it," she said at last.

"What are we going to call our costume in the contest?" asked Caroline. "Just 'shrub'?"

"Something that will appeal to the principal," Eddie said. She thoughtfully chewed her lip. "*I've* got it. 'A natural habitat'! That's what we'll call ourselves."

By the time they had put the sticks in the garage, Mother was standing at the door waiting for them: "I've made a pie for the Hatfords, and I want you girls to take it over," she said. "Just give it to whoever answers the door. Tell them it's in appreciation for the boys washing our windows. I've put it in this old hatbox and stuck a note inside."

"You've got to be kidding," said Eddie.

"Why would I be kidding?" Mother looked at her curiously. "You know, there are times I think I haven't raised you girls right. Maybe people just aren't as neighborly in Ohio, but here in West Virginia you show people you're grateful when they do something for you. It's the least we can do."

"I'll bet they throw it in the river," murmured Caroline.

"Throw it in the river! Why in the world would they do that?"

Caroline didn't even get a chance to tell Mother she was to be Goblin Queen in the fourth-grade play, because moments later she was crossing the swinging bridge, her sisters beside her, carrying the old hatbox with Mother's pumpkin chiffon pie inside it.

Eight

•

Pumpkin Chiffon

"Look!" said Josh.

Wally looked where his brother was pointing. On the bank, across the river, Caroline and her sisters were down by the water gathering sticks.

The boys moved behind some wild rhododendron and watched.

"What do you suppose they're up to?" asked Jake.

Josh turned to Wally. "Your class isn't doing a project with sticks, is it?"

Wally shook his head.

"Maybe they're going to have a fire in their fireplace," suggested Peter.

"The Bensons left them stacks and stacks of wood," Jake told him. "This has got to be something else. What do you think, Wally?"

Wally watched the girls without answering. He

72

watched them holding the sticks up in the air, sort of like poles for a tepee.

"A tepee," he said.

"That's *it*!" cried Jake. "Wally, you're a genius! They're going to come to the Halloween parade as a tepee and Indians! Eddie will probably be the tepee and Beth and Caroline will be the chief and squaw."

"Wow!" said Peter admiringly.

Wally felt sick. The Malloys would win for sure. *No*body had ever entered the parade before as a tepee and Indians. How could they ever top that?

"How can we top that?" asked Josh.

"We don't *have* to top it!" Jake answered. "All we have to do is stop it. All we have to do is dress up like something that would naturally knock down a tepee. *Think*, everybody!"

"A train?" said Peter.

"Not a train, dum-dum."

"A car?"

"Peter, we're talking Old West here, way back before there *were* any cars. C'mon, Wally. What could it be?"

Wally tried to remember pictures he'd seen in his history book, in the chapter called "Westward, Ho!"

"Buffalo," he said.

"That's it!" cried Jake. "We're buffalo. We don't have to be vultures after all. Josh, you've got to design some new costumes."

The boys went on home and made milk shakes in the kitchen to celebrate.

"I didn't *think* they'd be a centipede," Josh said. "I'll bet they whispered that just loud enough for Peter to hear so it would throw us off. They probably knew already they were going to be a tepee and Indians."

"All this time they've probably been working on their costumes—the chief's headdress and everything—while we were trying to find something that looked like vultures' claws," said Josh.

Ding dong.

Jake had just turned off the blender and was pouring the thick shake into glasses when the doorbell rang.

"Don't anybody take a drink of mine," Wally warned as he went to the door and opened it.

There stood Caroline and her sisters holding a hatbox.

"Mom sent this over," Caroline said, holding out the box. "It's a pumpkin pie."

Wally could not believe this was happening. The girls didn't look as though they liked this any more than he did, but Wally couldn't be sure.

"Who is it, Wally?" called Jake.

"A pie," said Wally.

"*Who?*"

Peter came running to the doorway and stared down through the cellophane top of the hatbox. "It's a pumpkin pie!" he said.

"Enjoy," said Eddie, and the girls turned and walked away.

"Don't forget to return the plate," Beth called over her shoulder.

All four boys were standing at the door now.

"I don't think their mom baked this at all," said Josh. "I'll bet there's a trick to it."

"That's what they thought when they threw our cake in the river," Wally reminded him.

"Just the same, I'll bet it's made of dog doo or something. I'll bet the girls are ticked off because of what I drew on the back of my math paper." Josh stared hard at the pie.

Wally opened the lid and took a cautious sniff. "Sure doesn't smell like dog doo."

"I still think there's something gross in it. Like centipedes. Bugs of some kind."

They took the pie to the kitchen and Wally lifted it out of the box. He accidentally let go of one side too soon, and it fell to the table with a plop. A large crack appeared on the top of the pie.

"Hoo boy!" said Wally.

"It's okay. That will give us a chance to see if

there's anything in the middle of it," said Jake. He got out Mother's magnifying glass and held it over the crack in the pie.

"See anything?" asked Wally.

"Not yet. Give me a butter knife."

Wally handed him a knife, and Jake probed gently down into the crack, then pulled the knife out and looked at the pumpkin coating it. "Looks okay, but I wouldn't be too sure."

"They probably wouldn't have stuck anything right in the middle of it," Josh said. "If I were going to put something gross in a pie, I'd stick it along the edge of the crust where you wouldn't think to look."

Jake took the knife and probed every few inches near the edge of the pie. With a spoon he lifted out a little bit of pumpkin chiffon here and a little there, examining it closely. It appeared to be only pumpkin.

"We still ought to taste it," he said. "It still could be made with pee. Who wants the first taste?"

"Not me!" said Wally.

"Don't look at me," said Josh.

Everyone turned to Peter.

"You always make me do everything!" Peter wailed.

"Oh, I'll take the first bite," said Jake. He lifted

the spoon to his lips and touched it first with his tongue. Then he actually put some in his mouth and rolled it around a moment, swallowing. "I'll be darned," he said. "It's good."

"Let me see," said Josh. Another bite. "You're right. It's great!"

"Give me some," said Peter, jabbing a spoon down right in the middle and lifting out a large bite.

And then Wally saw the note stuck to the bottom of the box. "Oh, no!" he said.

Dear Ellen—

Just wanted you to know how much we appreciated your boys washing our windows. There is such a wonderful sense of community here. Thank you so much for helping us to feel at home. Hope you enjoy my pumpkin chiffon pie—it's my great-aunt's recipe, and sort of a tradition at our house in October.

Cordially,

Jean Malloy

"Oh, brother!" said Josh.

"We," added Jake, "are in big trouble."

They stared down at the pie, which looked as though squirrels had been walking through it in golf shoes. Bites had been taken out of it here and there.

"Mom will *kill* us if she sees this!" said Wally. Mother always said that a gift of food should be enjoyed three ways: first with the eyes, then with the nose, and finally, with the mouth. If someone went to all the work to bake something for you, you should admire it first as an artistic creation, and not just gobble it down.

"What are we going to tell her?" Josh murmured.

"That we were digging for dog doo?" said Peter.

"There's only one thing to do," Jake decided. "Eat the pie. Then we've got to go to Ethel's Bakery and buy another. We'll put it in the box with the note and leave it on the table, and Mom won't know the difference. We'll take the plate back to Mrs. Malloy and tell her that Mom said thanks."

The boys ate the pie, more out of duty than pleasure—not because it wasn't good, but because they didn't seem so hungry anymore.

Afterward, Wally went upstairs to shake money out of his bank and wondered how life could get so complicated. Unfortunately, all the money he had was in a clay piggy bank that Aunt Ida had given him last Christmas, and the only way anyone could get money out was to shake it upside down and hope that something would fall out of the slot, though it hardly ever did.

He sat on his bed and shook and shook. How could it be that with so many dimes and nickels and pennies in it, hardly any ever hit the slot in exactly the right way to fall out? If one coin fell out every ten minutes, and there were a hundred and seventy-nine coins, then how long would it take before . . . ?

"*Hurry*, Wally! We have to be home in a half hour. We need to buy that pie before Mom gets here, and we've only got five dollars between us. We'll need more than that."

Wally took a hammer, smashed his clay piggy bank to smithereens, scooped up the money, and gave it to Jake.

•

The boys were all in the other room quietly watching TV when their mother walked in the back door and clunked her purse and keys on the kitchen counter.

"What's this?" Wally heard her say.

There was a silence—a long, long silence. The sound of a box being opened. The squeak of the kitchen floor. Then a long, slow "I de-clare!"

Wally held his breath.

"I de-clare!" Mother said again.

Wally couldn't stand it. Neither could Jake or Josh or Peter. They all went to the door of the kitchen.

"Well, now I've seen everything!" Mother said, staring down into the box and holding Mrs. Malloy's note in her hand.

"I don't see anything," said Wally.

"Did this just come this afternoon?" Mother asked, pointing to the box.

Wally nodded. "Caroline and her sisters brought it over."

Mother stood shaking her head. "Jean Malloy says in her note that she baked this pumpkin chiffon pie herself from her great-aunt's recipe, and this pie came from Ethel's Bakery, or I'll eat the box."

Wally almost choked.

"H-how do you know?" asked Jake.

"Because Ethel's the only one who sprinkles caramel and pecans around the rim of her pumpkin pies. And what's more, she always leaves a little swirl of filling right in the middle, sort of a trademark, you might say. I saw these pies in her window just this morning, and Jean Malloy's got the nerve to tell me she made it herself."

Hoo boy! Wally thought, and his legs felt like rubber. Maybe they should tell her. Maybe they

80

should just come right out and tell her that when she sent that chocolate cake over to Mrs. Malloy in August, Caroline thought it was a trick and threw it in the river, so the boys thought maybe this was a trick, and they were just trying to dig around and see if there was any dog doo in it. . . . But then he thought of how awful Mom would feel if she knew her beautiful cake had gone in the river. She'd want to know *why* Caroline would suspect such a thing, and then he'd have to tell her all the ways the Hatford boys and the Malloy girls had been tormenting each other since the Malloys arrived. No, he had better keep quiet.

"If the woman doesn't bake, it's not a sin," Mother went on. "Why couldn't she just have said she'd picked up a pie for our dinner and hoped we'd enjoy it? Why did she have to say she baked it herself? And then, to call it pumpkin chiffon, when pumpkin chiffon pie is at least two inches high. If this is the way they do things in Ohio, I'm glad I don't live in Ohio. Boys, wash up. We're having dinner soon."

Nine

•

Thank-you Note

It was when Caroline was brushing her teeth the next morning that Wally returned the plate. She had been standing in front of the mirror practicing her lines for the play—"Wait, little elf. Maybe your idea is a good one! Maybe it *would* be more fun to do *good* tricks this Halloween and surprise the village people!"—when she heard the doorbell.

"Why, good morning, Wally!" came her father's voice. "Or is it Jake or Josh or Peter? I'm never sure."

"I'm Wally," came a second voice. "I just wanted to return Mrs. Malloy's pie plate and tell her thank you very much. The pumpkin chiffon pie was delicious!"

"I'll be sure to tell her," Father said. "Jean makes it every year. I like a big piece after a football game. Provided we win, of course."

Caroline came down after she heard the door close.

"Well, *now* maybe we're all friends again," Mother said to her. "One of the Hatford boys returned my pie plate and said the pie was delicious, so I guess they really enjoyed it. Let's try and keep things this way, huh? Stay friends?"

"Why not?" said Caroline. At the moment Wally and his brothers were the last thing on her mind. It was the play that was important. Never mind that the fifth and sixth grades wouldn't see it. The others would, along with all their teachers, and people would remember her, so that when they were looking for someone to play a starring role in fifth or sixth—

"Good grief! Have some bread with your peanut butter!" Mother said, watching Caroline make her lunch. "You have enough peanut butter on that bread for three sandwiches, Caroline. Pay attention."

"Dost thou talk to thy queen in such a manner?" Caroline asked, raising one eyebrow.

"I dost," said Mother. "And don't forget to pack some carrots and celery, m'lady."

·

"Well, class, we've got one week to the Halloween play," Miss Applebaum said, facing the fourth graders in her apple-red dress. "I still need three more boys, however, and if I don't get any volunteers, I'm going to have to volunteer for you. Come on, now. It'll be fun. Your audience is only little kids, after all. Don't let it scare you. If you forget a line, so what? It's not the end of the world."

Finally one hand went up, then another.

"Okay, I've got everyone we need except a footman, and we need somebody strong. Wally Hatford, I choose you. Lunch-hour rehearsal. Don't forget."

Wally Hatford! A footman! Right! thought Caroline.

When she stood on the stage at lunchtime, Caroline remembered that the last time she was here, having sneaked in after lunch, Wally and some of the other fourth-grade boys had sneaked in, too, unknown to her, and were sitting in the dark in the back row, listening to her read a beautiful passage from *The Wind in the Willows*. But now she was supposed to be here, with the lights shining down on her, and Miss Applebaum smiling in the second row, and sometimes, when Miss Applebaum was showing someone else where to stand, or how to gesture when he talked, Caroline tipped back her head and studied all the ropes and pulleys and lights and switches and knew that this was where she belonged, that she was doing what she was born to do.

There was only one line, at the very end of the play, where someone had a better part than Caroline. That was when the Fairy Godmother of All the Woods and Glades came to the Goblin Queen and said, "Isabelle, all these years your hair has been matted and your skin has been wrinkled and rough, and your toes and fingers crooked, because you have looked the way you have lived. But because of these fine deeds you have performed this Halloween, you have shown the village people that beneath your dirty hair and crooked smile, there is indeed a heart of gold." Whereupon she touched the Goblin Queen with her magic wand, and flung off the ugly mask that Caroline would have been wearing, to reveal the true beauty beneath.

For just that one moment Caroline would have liked to be the Fairy Godmother of All the Woods and Glades, but she couldn't be both. And besides, right after that, her two footmen were supposed to help her sit down, and say, "Your throne, m'lady." And when she said, "Call the other goblins, that we may celebrate a Halloween of Good Deeds," Wally would say, "I hear, my Queen, and obey."

When Wally came to those lines, however, his face turned red and he looked as though he had a mouth full of rocks. He looked as though he would rather choke than say them.

"Who are you talking to, Wally, the floor?" Miss Applebaum called from her seat in the second row. "Speak up—look at Caroline when you talk. Don't mumble."

"I can't remember the lines, I'm not any good at this," Wally told her.

"Pish-posh!" said their teacher. "You only have two lines to say in the whole play, Wally. Come on, now. I know you can do it. Besides, if you forget a line, just make one up. Actors and actresses have to do that all the time."

"I hear, my Queen, and obey," Wally said finally, and started off the stage to call the other goblins.

Does life ever get better than this? Caroline wondered happily.

·

Fall was perhaps the favorite season in the Malloy family. Father was happiest when football had really begun; Mother liked it when the long, hot days of summer were over at last; Eddie liked any season that was warm enough for her to stand outside and bounce a ball off the side of the garage; and Beth liked autumn especially because all the books that had been taken from the library for summer reading had been returned, and she had a much better selection to choose from, especially her favorite books, such as *The Spider's Sting, Mark of the Mummy,* and *Scorpion People.* But the seasons of the year meant absolutely nothing to Caroline as long as she was onstage.

She and Beth and Eddie had just come back from the homecoming parade on Saturday and were raking leaves when Mr. Hatford came up the sidewalk with their mail.

"Hello, girls," he said. "Your dad must have been mighty pleased the way his team beat Wheeling last night. Nice to have a winning team for a change." He grinned as he walked up the steps. "So how are you all doing?"

"Fine," they answered together.

Caroline took a chance: "How are the guys coming with their Halloween costumes?"

Mr. Hatford scratched his head. "Come to think of it, I haven't heard a word out of them the past few days. All I get from Wally is griping about some danged play."

Caroline grinned, but Eddie put down her rake: "Aren't they even going to *be* in the parade?"

"I imagine so. Just don't hear them talk much about it, that's all."

Not much help from him, Caroline thought after he had gone. Was it possible the boys had just given up?

Leaves fell down around them, and Caroline stretched her arms toward the sky and said, "Life's wonderful! The Goblin Queen is in her glory! I never want to go back to Ohio again. I want to stay right here and become known in Buckman, and someday, in the concrete outside the school, they will put a marker for me with my name on it, saying, CAROLINE LENORE MALLOY FIRST APPEARED ONSTAGE IN THIS SCHOOL." Her sisters groaned.

The screen door slammed and Mother came down the steps: "Girls, look at this and tell me what you think. I just got a note from Mrs. Hatford, and this is what she said:

'Dear Mrs. Malloy:

If you hadn't said you made that pie yourself, I would have sworn it came from Ethel's Bakery. Thank you so much. It was delicious.

Ellen Hatford'

Is that an insult or a compliment? I can't even tell."

"She thinks you bought the pie?" asked Eddie.
"It certainly sounds that way to me."
"So isn't that a compliment?" asked Caroline.
"Not to me it's not. Not when it was Great-

Aunt Minna's recipe. Maybe she's just trying to take me down a peg—my bragging on about that recipe as I did. Oh, dear heaven! People were so much easier to get along with back in Ohio!"

After Mother went back in the house, Beth whispered, "What do you think happened to the pie? You don't think they threw it in the river, do you?"

"Well, *something* happened to it, or they wouldn't have bought a store pie and tried to pass it off as homemade. I'm sure that's exactly what happened too," Eddie said.

"Maybe it was just so good that once they took a taste, they kept eating and couldn't stop," Caroline suggested.

"I doubt it," said Eddie.

•

At school on Monday, Caroline leaned forward and whispered, "Wal-ly. Mom wants her pie back."

Miss Applebaum was over in one corner helping a group with a geography assignment.

Wally turned around. "What?"

"She says that since you didn't give it to your mother, she wants it back."

Wally stared.

"Well?" said Caroline.

"Well, nothing! We ate it!"

"Your mother didn't."

"How do you know?"

"The Goblin Queen knows all."

"Drop dead," said Wally.

"If we win the costume contest, you'll have to say, 'I hear, my Queen, and obey,' for a whole month. Did you ever think of that?"

"And if *we* win . . . ?"

Miss Applebaum turned around. "I hear people talking. Is that you, Caroline? Caroline and Wally? Suppose you share it with the class."

"Just practicing our lines, Miss Applebaum," Caroline said sweetly.

Ten

•

The Grand Finale

The buffalo costumes were not working out. Even Josh, the artist in the family, could not make brown grocery sacks look like the shaggy heads of buffalo, no matter how much stuff he glued on them. Every time he changed them still again and showed them to Mother, she'd say, "Is that a goat? No, wait. I've got it—a sheepdog."

"Why don't we just forget the girls and do something we think will win?" said Wally.

But Jake had other ideas. "What we need is a costume the teachers will like and the principal will love, that can still destroy anything in its path. Then no matter *what* the Malloys come up with, we can devour it."

"*Think*, Wally!" said Josh. "Think of something that can sort of suck up everything in its path."

"A vacuum cleaner," said Wally.

"Naw. What else?"

"A tidal wave."

"Yeah, what else?"

"A tornado."

"Keep thinking."

"An amoeba," said Wally.

"C'mon, Wally, *think*!"

Wally closed his eyes tight and thought so hard, his eyebrows hurt. "An alien spaceship," he said at last.

"That's it!" cried Jake. "We'll be aliens!"

"They can do anything!" said Josh. "We could get one of those huge truck inner tubes, and all of us could stand inside the middle, holding it up around our waists, and we'd knock over everything we bumped into! I'll design our helmets. . . ." He reached for his sketch pad and began. All you had to do was give Josh an idea, and he was already drawing a picture of it in his head.

"Wow," said Peter softly, as he watched the alien spaceship appearing right at the end of Josh's pencil.

When they asked their dad if he could get a giant inner tube for them, Mr. Hatford answered, "Why, I think that could be arranged."

At last everything seemed to be working out. The Halloween parade was only four days off, but meanwhile Wally had another worry. The play. *The Goblin Queen.* Caroline Malloy, in particular.

The trouble with Caroline was that she never stopped being queen. If she was eating lunch, she set her empty milk carton on top of her head like a crown and kept it there. If she had to go to the blackboard to explain a problem, she always picked up Miss Applebaum's pointer and used it like a scepter, anointing a knight. And she would slowly, regally, make her way up and down staircases, back straight, head high, looking neither to the right nor left.

To Wally there was nothing worse than being in a play with Caroline Malloy. Never mind that he would be doing something special for the younger students. He did not *want* to make primary children happy. The primary children were happy enough as it was. Wally wanted his recesses back. He wanted his lunch hour back. He did not want to spend them standing around a drafty stage waiting for Caroline Malloy to decide that playing good tricks at Halloween was better than playing bad ones. Whoever wrote that play was an idiot. It took thirty minutes for the Goblin Queen to get the point and the Fairy Godmother to make her beautiful, just so Wally could say, "Your throne, m'lady," and then, "I hear, my Queen, and obey."

Each day of practice got longer and longer because Caroline kept ad-libbing her part. If her line was "What do you suppose, dear sisters, the villagers would do if we were to *wash* their windows for a change?" Caroline would say, "What do you suppose, my dear, dear goblin sisters, the villagers would do if, instead of causing them trouble and hardship, we did something kind instead, such as washing their windows?"

Wally would stand on one foot and then the other, and finally even Miss Applebaum grew tired: "Caroline, if we don't hurry this play along, our primary students will all be asleep before we're done."

And finally Caroline would say, "We must spread the word throughout the Goblin Kingdom, that there will be the kind of tricks on Halloween night that will make it a night to remember and fill all hearts with joy." Then and only then could Wally escort her to her chair and say, "Your throne, m'lady."

·

When Thursday came, Wally wasn't sure whether he wanted to get up or not. It was the day of the play, which was a good reason to stay in bed. On the other hand, once it was over, he'd never have to do that part again, which was the only reason he could think of to get up at all.

He turned over on his back and noticed a narrow shaft of sunlight coming through his window, illuminating the dust particles in the beam. It was as though the beam were full of dust and the rest of the room was clear. If air was always so dusty, he wondered, did you inhale a big wad of dust every time you breathed? Were your lungs like a dust mop? Was that why people sneezed, to shake out their lungs? Was that—?

"Wally, are you up?" Mother called from below. "If you want pancakes, you'd better come now."

Wally, the footman, got out of bed, pulled on his jeans and socks, and gave a big sigh.

At school the primary students filed into the auditorium about ten o'clock, and the students from Miss Applebaum's class who were in the play gathered behind the velvet curtain onstage.

"I can't believe this is really happening," Caroline said to Wally, both of them wearing their goblin cloaks and hoods. "I'm a real actress at last. Do you know where you'll see my name someday?"

"On a tombstone?" said Wally.

Caroline flashed him a disgusted look. "In lights! On Broadway! Someday you and your brothers will go to the movies and see me up there on the screen."

"If we see you on the screen, we'll ask for our money back," Wally told her.

Beyond the velvet curtain the audience had grown quiet, and Wally could hear Miss Applebaum telling them about the play. And then the music started, the lights went out, there was the sound of the curtain being pulled apart, and Caroline was walking onstage followed by five other goblins.

"Halloween again!" Caroline was saying. "I wish we could do something different this year, don't you? I'm getting tired of the same old thing." And the play began.

If it wasn't for Caroline, Wally might have enjoyed the play—a little bit, anyway. It was sort of fun peeping out from behind the curtain to see the younger children watching, Peter with his eyes wide and his mouth open. To hear them laugh at all the funny lines, and giggle when one of the witches tripped over her broomstick on purpose and went sprawling.

He and another boy had to pull the curtain between the first and second acts, too, and that was fun. It was also fun to watch the custodian sitting on a stool offstage, making the lights get brighter or more dim.

But Caroline, as usual, had to ruin it all. She added lines that weren't there. She added words to the lines that were. Even Miss Applebaum in the first row was trying to get Caroline's attention to hurry her along. Finally, when it came time for Wally to say his line, he felt he could not stand it any longer.

"Your throne, m'lady," he said, escorting her to the chair, and then, just as Caroline sat down, he pulled it backward and Caroline sat down on the floor with a plop.

The primary children shrieked with laughter, and even Miss Applebaum, who looked horrified at first, seemed to be trying very hard not to laugh.

Wally had thought that would be the end of it. He had thought that Caroline would be so embarrassed that she would want the play to be over quickly.

But Caroline was not hurrying her lines. She was not even getting up. The children stopped laughing. Miss Applebaum leaned forward, looking concerned.

And then, from the floor where she lay with her arms outstretched, Caroline said grandly, "Where are my good and faithful footmen? I am more exhausted than I knew. Please bear me thither, that I might lie among the flowers of the field, surrounded by my people." And she folded her arms across her chest.

Wally stared at Caroline and then at the other

footman. They looked at Miss Applebaum, who was nodding to them.

There was nothing else to be done. "I hear, my Queen, and obey," Wally said.

He picked Caroline up by the arms. The other footman picked her up by the feet. And as they carried her offstage, Caroline turned toward the audience and blew them a kiss. Everyone clapped. It made Wally sick to his stomach.

•

That evening the boys tried out their spaceship costume. Mr. Hatford had gone to a truck stop near Elkins and bought a bigger inner tube than the boys even knew existed. All four of them could easily fit in the center hole, one hand holding the inner tube up, the other carrying the space guns that Josh had designed out of aluminum foil. Each of them was facing a different direction, and with the strange helmets Josh had designed, also of foil, they looked like men from another planet. Josh had even made green paper ears that fit over their own.

"Well, if you don't win first prize, you should get a prize for originality," their father told them, as the boys practiced moving about the living room, two walking sideways, one walking backward, and Jake in front, leading the way. Naturally

Jake. It was Wally's idea, yet Jake was always the General.

When Mother came home from the hardware store at nine, the boys showed her their spaceship, and she said it was the best costume they'd ever made, absolutely.

As she hung up her coat, however, Wally heard her say to his father, "Tom, are the Malloys raising chickens?"

"Chickens? I'd think the coach would have enough to do without fooling with chickens. Why?"

"Because the Malloy girls were in the hardware store the other day buying chicken wire, and I just wondered."

"What?" yelled Wally, and slipped out from under the giant inner tube.

The other boys crawled out, too, and the inner tube landed with a loud *whap* on the floor.

Mrs. Hatford turned around. "Wally, don't yell. I simply asked if the Malloys were raising chickens."

Jake and Josh stared at her openmouthed.

"What did I *say*?" Mrs. Hatford looked around her. "It's not as though I announced the Second Coming! All I said was that the Malloy girls were in the store to—"

"How *much* wire?" asked Jake.

"Why, I don't know . . . quite a lot, as I remember, but it isn't our best grade at all. It was that bendable stuff that will sag if even a cat jumps on it."

"Their *costume!*" cried Wally.

"They aren't going to be a tepee at all, I'll bet!" said Josh. "Think, Mom! Did they buy anything else? *Say* anything? *Do* anything?"

"What's got into you boys? The youngest one stood there wrapping it around and around herself, while the older sisters were paying for it, but I figured she was just being a bit silly, and . . ."

The boys huddled around the kitchen table.

"What do you suppose it could be?" asked Josh.

"Something awesome, I'll bet," said Wally.

"There's only one thing to do," said Jake, when the others turned toward him. "Smash it."

Eleven

•

Izzie

The "natural habitat" had simply not worked. Murphy's Five and Dime didn't carry the little birds and things the girls had wanted to tie to the branches. And when Caroline, Beth, and Eddie were all bound together to make the trunk, it was hard to walk. They finally decided on a lizard made out of chicken wire.

"The principal has a terrarium in his office," Eddie remembered, "with a lizard and stuff. I even know the name of the lizard—Izzie, he calls it. Why don't we be a lizard and wear a collar that says IZZIE?"

So they bought some chicken wire at the hardware store, fashioned it into a huge lizard in three sections, one for each of them, then spent the evening before the parade tacking green cloth over it, using buttons for eyes, and printing IZZIE on a collar to go around its huge neck.

When Caroline awoke the next morning, she decided that life was more wonderful in Buckman than she had ever imagined. The day before, she had been a Goblin Queen, and today she was the hindquarters of a giant lizard. She made her parents laugh by waddling around in her part of the costume, sticking out one leg, then the other.

Coach Malloy carefully tied the lizard forms to the roof of his car and drove them to school. As the girls carried them in on their heads, they saw the Hatford boys stop in their tracks and stare.

"You guys still in the parade, or do you just want to give up now?" Eddie asked, as they arranged the sections in the proper order.

"Why don't you just promise to be our obedient slaves and get it over with?" said Beth.

"Whatever you've thought of, I'll bet it can't top this," said Caroline.

And she saw Peter look up at Wally. "We can't, can we?" he asked, and Caroline and her sisters smiled.

Why didn't the boys stop trying to drive them out of Buckman? Caroline wondered. That trick Wally had pulled on her during the play really backfired when he had to carry her out. *Everyone* had cheered for her. She was the Goblin Queen to end all Goblin Queens, and Wally had only created a scene that was even better.

"The contest isn't over yet," said Jake.

"It hasn't even started," Peter said.

"Don't count your chickens . . . uh, lizards . . . before they're hatched," said Wally.

•

It was hard to keep their minds on their studies that morning. Wally seemed nervous as a cat in a doghouse, Caroline thought, and it was strange to know that with a mother who worked in a hardware store, the Hatford boys couldn't have thought up something original themselves.

At noon the lunchroom was buzzing with chatter about the afternoon, and when the bell rang at one, all students who were going to enter the contest in groups were allowed to get ready.

Caroline went to the rest room, her last chance before she became a lizard, then hurried out into the hallway. She stopped, for there, disappearing around a corner, was a huge giant inner tube, propelled by the Hatford brothers, all wearing strange alien helmets and carrying space guns. The boys even had green paper ears. It was a *wonderful* costume! They'd win for sure.

No sooner had the aliens disappeared, however, than Eddie came racing down the hall, fire in her eyes.

"Where are they?" Eddie was saying, Beth at her heels. "Where are they?"

"Who?"

"The Hatford goons, that's who," said Eddie. "Did you see what they did to Izzie?"

Caroline ran down the hall and looked. Izzie the Lizard was flat as a slice of cheese.

"Them?" cried Caroline.

"Them!" said Beth.

"Students who are entering the parade singly, please stay in your classrooms until your room is called," came a voice over the loudspeaker. "Students who are part of a group costume, please line up in the hall."

"We'll worry about the boys later," said Beth. "Come on, Eddie, and help me bend this wire back into shape again. If we hurry we can fix up Izzie again before the parade starts."

"I'm going to fix *them*!" Eddie declared. "I don't know when or where, but they're not getting away with this. That's fighting dirty. They're so afraid we'll win the contest they can't stand it."

"We were ready to smash their pumpkins," Beth reminded her, and nobody spoke for a while. With the three of them working, it didn't take long to fix Izzie. Once they got their hands inside the chicken wire frame, they were able to shape the lizard the way it had been, and gradually the legs and head and body emerged, good as new.

But Caroline felt a part coming on, as actresses sometimes do. The alien spaceship had become a loathsome dragon, and only she, the fair and lovely maiden, could destroy it. While everyone waited in the hall for the parade to begin, she slipped out of her section of the chicken wire costume and into her empty classroom.

Opening her desk, she got out her new scissors, the best scissors she had ever had, scissors that had points as long and as sharp as an alligator's tooth. And then, aware of nothing else but the role she was destined to play, she walked down the line of costumes in the hall—past the troop of clowns, past the flowers in a pot, the swarm of bees, the deck of cards, the acrobats, until she saw the alien spaceship up ahead.

And then, the fair and lovely maiden faced the dragon, and, taking a deep breath, cast her eyes heavenward for courage. Holding the scissors in both hands over her head like a dagger, she ran forward and plunged the sharp points into the side of the giant inner tube, using all the strength she could muster.

BANG!

It was an explosion. Somehow Caroline had thought that the air would slowly leak out. Somehow she had thought it might be more like a soft hiss.

She fell backward, as Jake, Josh, Wally, and Peter stared down at the strip of black rubber that lay around their feet.

The next thing she knew, she was being led to the principal's office, Beth on one side of her for support, Eddie on the other, while the four Hatford brothers, still in shock, brought up the rear.

Twelve

•

Letters

What happened was that neither the Hatfords nor the Malloys won the contest. Both groups were disqualified because the boys had smashed the lizard to begin with, and Caroline had destroyed the spaceship.

Instead, five kids who were dressed up like instruments in a symphony orchestra won first place, and if *they* had been in on the bargain, both the Hatfords and Malloys would have been taking orders from a violin, a viola, a clarinet, a bassoon, and an oboe.

The girls had seemed almost relieved at the verdict. At least they didn't have to worry about being anyone's slaves, Wally thought. And maybe in a way he and his brothers were glad it was over, too, because they didn't want to be slaves, either, but they *had* had big plans for that inner tube on the river next summer. *That's* what hurt.

The boys stayed at school just long enough to drink some cider and eat some doughnuts at the Halloween party after the parade, but then they slipped away and headed home. It was the first Halloween they could remember that they had not been in the parade.

"This is absolutely, totally, all-out war," said Jake. "They ruined all the fun we could have had with that inner tube next summer, and for what? It didn't take them long to put their costume back together. We smashed it, but we didn't *destroy* it."

"We wanted to, though," Wally reminded him, but Jake paid no attention whatsoever.

"You know what I'd like to do to those girls? Trap them in the cemetery."

Wally looked quickly over at Jake as they slouched along the sidewalk toward home.

"*Then* what?" asked Wally.

"I don't know. That would probably be enough. They'd be scared out of their skin."

Would it never end? Wally wondered. When they were eighty-five-year-old men, would they still be trying to get even with three old women named Malloy? He could see it now: when Eddie, Beth, and Caroline each graduated from high school, the Hatford brothers would have to attend just so they could boo when a Malloy walked across the stage.

When each of the Malloy girls married, the Hatford brothers would go just so they could tie junk on the backs of their cars. Wherever the Malloy girls went, the Hatfords would forever follow just to make them miserable.

"Why don't we just forget them!" Wally said. "Tomorrow night's Halloween. Just forget them, and go trick-or-treating like we used to. If the Bensons were here, we'd be starting out about six o'clock, and we wouldn't stop till close to ten. We were always the first ones out on the street and the last ones in. Man, we'd get so much loot, we'd have enough candy to last all year."

"No matter what we do, we'll probably run into Beth or Caroline or Eddie," Jake said disgust-edly. "They're *every*where!"

"They'll figure out some way to ruin Hallow-een for us," said Josh. "I wish we could just lock them up on Halloween night and have the town to ourselves."

"Fat chance," said Wally.

There was a letter waiting for them when they got home. It was a letter to Wally from his friend Bill Benson:

Dear Wally (and Josh and Jake and Peter):

We were making plans for Halloween the other day and wondered what you guys are doing this year. Man, we used to have fun, didn't we? Remember the time we soaped the windows of the principal's car? And the scavenger hunt in the cemetery? Remember the ghost-walk we had at our party when everyone was blindfolded and had to eat a spoonful of guts (spaghetti) and eyeballs (peeled grapes)?

I don't know whether we'll be going out trick-or-treating or not, because there are at least two parties going on. Maybe we'll go to both.

Tony's teacher (the "Georgia Peach") is going to come to school on Halloween dressed as a belly dancer. That's what she said, anyway. If she does, all us guys are going to be sitting in the first row, I know that. She probably won't, though.

Mom really likes it down here. She's got a part-time job in a bookstore, and I think she'd sort of like to stay. Dad doesn't know yet whether he wants to stay or not. Same with us. We really miss you guys, but Georgia's great too.

Anything happening there since we left? The Malloys taking good care of our house? They better not mess up the walls in our bedrooms with girl stuff.

Write when you can.

Bill (and Danny, Steve, Tony, and Doug)

Dear Bill (and Danny, Steve, Tony, and Doug):

Tomorrow's Halloween and you know how many parties we've been invited to? None. Zero. Today we were disqualified from the Halloween contest because we smashed the Malloys' chicken-wire lizard and flattened it like a pancake. It didn't make that much difference, because they got it back in shape by the time the parade began, but you know what Crazy Caroline did? Do you know how nuts she really is? Punctured our inner-tube spaceship with a pair of scissors. It exploded like a paper bag. Then they got disqualified. Jake's up in his room trying to think of a way to get even. If you guys don't come back pretty soon, we are going to spend all our time thinking up ways to get even, and they are going to think up ways to get even, and if this goes on for a whole year, we'll go nuts.

Don't fall in love with your teacher, even if she does dress up like a belly dancer. Don't fall in love with Georgia either. Tell your mom she can get a job in the bookstore here.

I mean it, you guys!

Wally (and Jake and Josh and Peter)

"I've got it!"

Jake came into Wally's room, where he was

just sealing his letter to Bill Benson. Josh and Peter followed him in, Peter still eating a peppermint patty he had found in his jeans pocket but had sat on, and it was as flat as a fifty-cent piece.

"What?" Wally asked.

"Something Bill said in his letter. About all the parties the guys were going to, and the scavenger hunt in the cemetery. Let's invite the girls to a party."

"Are you *nuts*?" cried Wally.

"No, let's invite them to a party. Just not *here*."

"What are you talking about?" asked Josh.

"We'll invite them to a party at some girl's house, but they'll have to go through the cemetery to get there."

Wally thought it over. "They'll never go."

"Sure they will. They can't resist."

"And then?" asked Josh.

"We'll think of something," Jake told him.

·

The boys spent the evening on the invitation. Jake and Josh even went to the drugstore and bought a pack of party invitations, half price, just for the one they wanted to use. It had to look official.

It was the kind girls would send, all right. There was a border all the way around of tiny pumpkins, and a perky little witch stirring a kettle of something. On the inside it said:

> *Little witch has come to say,*
> *Ghosts and goblins like to play.*
> *Won't you come and join the fun?*
> *There'll be treats for everyone.*
> *Time* _____
> *Place* _____

"Barf! Vomit!" said Jake, when he read it to Wally.

Wally studied the invitation. "But what are you going to write at the bottom?"

"That's what we have to figure out," said Jake. "Who do the girls run around with besides each other?"

"Caroline runs around with the girl who played the fairy godmother in the play," said Wally.

"Nope. Has to be in the same class as Eddie. If it's any younger, Beth and Eddie won't go. *Think,* Josh!" Jake said. "Who does Eddie hang around with?"

"What about the girl who plays shortstop at recess?"

"Mary Ruth?" said Jake.

"Yeah."

"Where does she live?" asked Wally.

Josh looked at Jake, and started to grin. "Over near the cemetery."

"Perfect!" said Jake.

The boys gathered around the dining-room table while Jake filled out the invitation with Mother's pen.

Time: 8 *P.M. Halloween night (all-girl party)*
Place: *Mary Ruth Sayer's*
         409 Bremer Road
P.S.   *Meet at the north entrance to the cemetery, and bring a flashlight. Follow the clues.*

"What clues?" asked Peter.

"We'll have them posted all around the cemetery, right up to that bench by the stone wall in the Remembrance Garden," Jake told them. "When they get that far, we'll let them have it."

"Have what?" asked Peter.

"Worms," grinned Jake. "A bucket of worms. We'll be watching from the top of the wall, and as soon as they sit down, we dump."

Wally stared. "Do you know how long it takes to dig up a whole bucket of worms?"

"It will really be a bucket of spaghetti with a can of worms tossed in. There will be just enough worms wriggling about to make them think that it's all worms. They'll probably faint."

Peter sucked in his breath.

They spent the entire evening in Wally's room making a map of the cemetery and figuring out where to place the clues. Then, keeping the map for themselves, they put the invitation in its envelope and wrote, *Eddie, Beth, and Caroline* on the front. Just before going to bed Wally went across the swinging bridge beside Jake and Josh, and they silently dropped the envelope in the Malloys' mailbox.

Thirteen

•

Clues

"**G**irls," Mother said on Saturday, coming through the door with the mail in her hand, "it looks as though you got a party invitation. It's the right size, anyway."

Caroline, Beth, and Eddie were doing their Saturday chores. At the word *party* they all stopped their sweeping, dusting, and mopping and gathered around the small white envelope in Mother's hand.

"It didn't have a stamp, so someone must have hand-delivered it," Mother said, giving it to Eddie.

Eddie opened it up, and read aloud:

> *"Little witch has come to say,*
> *Ghosts and goblins like to play.*
> *Won't you come and join the fun?*
> *There'll be treats for everyone."*

"Yuk!" said Beth. "Who would send an invitation like that?"

Eddie stared at the name at the bottom. "It's Mary Ruth, from school! This doesn't sound like her."

"Maybe it's all she could find," said Mother. "Anyway, all three of you are invited."

Eddie kept reading. "It's tonight! The party starts at the cemetery and we have to follow clues. Now, that's more like it."

"And it's *all* girls!" said Beth.

"We won't even go trick-or-treating. We won't have to run into the boys," added Caroline.

"Maybe that's the way they do things here in West Virginia, deliver the invitation the day of the party," Mother said. "I think it's wonderful that you're making friends at school. Finish your work, and you can spend the rest of the day deciding on costumes."

The Malloy girls had always liked putting together their own costumes instead of buying them ready-made in the stores. Eddie decided to go as a football player, in one of Dad's old uniforms; Beth would go as a robot from outer space, with a stocking over her hair to make her look bald; and Caroline would wear her Goblin Queen costume from the play at school.

Caroline simply could not wait for the party to

begin, and when she heard Beth say that you went up one street to get to the cemetery, and Eddie saying no, you went up another, Caroline told them she would get on her bike and check it out.

It was almost five o'clock when Caroline left the house, and it was much colder then when they'd gone camping but still a beautiful October evening. Leaves fell down around her face and shoulders as she rode, and Caroline wondered if it ever got that beautiful in Ohio. Probably. She'd just never had as much fun back in Ohio as she did here, even though she *had* got herself and her sisters in trouble for stabbing the alien spaceship.

It wasn't all her fault, though. She never would have punctured their spaceship if they hadn't flattened Izzie. Why couldn't the Hatford boys be normal? Or was that normal for boys? She didn't know. Peter's only fault was that he was a Hatford. Wally might have turned out all right if he hadn't had Josh and Jake for brothers. It was the eleven-year-old twins she suspected of being the worst—Jake, for giving orders, and Josh, for the stuff he drew in his sketchbook.

She turned up a road at the edge of town. To the left of her were the gravestones of the Buckman cemetery—Eddie was right—and on up ahead she could see the big iron gate at the entrance. She began pedaling up the hill, but suddenly skidded to a stop, letting her bicycle tip, and fell over into a clump of weeds.

There, not thirty yards ahead, were Jake, Josh, and Wally, taping a piece of paper to the iron gate of the cemetery.

Them!

Caroline was torn between riding up to the boys and catching them in the act, or racing home to tell Beth and Eddie. She decided to stay put until the boys left, and as soon as they had gone through the gate and were out of sight, she pedaled home as fast as her feet would go.

She burst into the house and collapsed on the sofa, panting.

"Caroline?" said Beth, coming over.

Eddie clattered downstairs. "What's wrong?"

"Wait till you hear!" said Caroline, and told them that the boys had been taping something to the gate of the cemetery.

"Them!" cried Beth and Eddie together.

"I *wondered* why Mary Ruth didn't say anything in school yesterday about a party!" said Eddie. "Those dumb boys! Didn't they even think we might have called Mary Ruth to check it out?"

"But we didn't," Beth reminded her.

"You're right, we didn't. We almost fell for it. Well, there's only one thing to do. Go over to the cemetery now and see what they're up to."

They took a flashlight and headed up the street. When they got to the cemetery, there was the note the boys had taped to the gate: *Turn left and go to the first grave on the right.*

Beth and Caroline giggled. "They must think we're really stupid to fall for this," said Beth.

"But we would have if I hadn't seen them here," Caroline reminded her.

"Let's follow it and see what they were planning to do," said Eddie.

They soon found the tombstone, a stone pyramid, and there was a note taped to that: *Follow the winding drive to the fence.*

Cautiously the girls followed the winding drive, and when the beam of the flashlight fell on the fence, there, just as the instructions said, was another piece of paper: *Fifty steps to the right, then left to the shed.*

They found the shed. Still another note. *Follow the path on your left to the bench in the Remembrance Garden.*

"I don't like this," said Beth. "They're up to something, all right."

Quietly they followed the path until they came to a bench by a high stone wall, with rosebushes all around—probably a beautiful place in the summer, Caroline thought, but sinister-looking now in the moonlight.

Eddie shone the flashlight around. There was a note on the bench: *Sit here and wait for instructions*, it said.

"Oh, no, we don't," said Beth. "I'll bet it's wet paint." Gingerly she put out one hand and tested. Dry.

"They were probably going to jump out of the trees with masks on and scare us silly," said Caroline.

"Or throw water on us," said Beth. "Look how we'd have been trapped here in this corner, right up against the wall."

"Well, I think we ought to look around," said Eddie. They climbed the bank beside the wall, making their way through the bare rosebushes, until they had scrabbled to the top of the stone wall behind the bench.

"Eddie!" said Caroline. "Look here."

The girls stared at a pan sitting just behind the wall. It was an ordinary saucepan with a lid on it, as though someone had made a pot of stew and left it there to cool.

Slowly Caroline put out one hand and lifted the lid, as Eddie shone the light on it. "Spaghetti?" she said. And then she gave a little cry, because the spaghetti started to move.

"Worms!" gulped Beth.

"Spaghetti *and* worms!" said Eddie. "They

were going to *drop* them on us, I'll bet! They were going to be waiting right up there behind the wall, and as soon as we sat down on that bench, they were going to dump it on our heads!"

Caroline shivered with the thought. All three girls shivered.

"What are we going to do?" asked Beth.

"We are going to go home and leave the house again at five of eight, just as though we were going to a party," said Eddie. "Just in case they're watching. But after that . . ." She began to smile. "Trust me," she said, and took out a pen and paper.

Fourteen

•

Party

Jake, Josh, and Wally sat on the wall overlooking the bench in the Remembrance Garden, and watched for a beam of a flashlight that would tell them the girls were coming.

"I can't understand it," said Jake. "We saw them leave the house around eight, we followed them to the cemetery . . . we saw them start off with the first clue before we came over here. Where the heck could they be?"

"Peter was smart," said Josh. "He said he'd rather go trick-or-treating than get even with the girls. It's a good thing he didn't come. He'd never stop complaining."

"Well, you're doing a pretty good job of it yourself," grumbled Jake.

"Maybe they got lost and decided to go back," said Wally, feeling pretty cold and tired, too, and

123

certainly ready to give up and go trick-or-treating. They had wasted enough time as it was.

"I don't think so. Eddie wouldn't give up that easily," Jake told him. "They were so close! There were only four clues altogether!"

"But *they* didn't know there were only four. Maybe they thought they'd be here all night," said Wally.

The boys sat huddled together another three or four minutes, scanning the dark cemetery for any sign of a light.

"Well, I don't know what happened to them, but this is a lousy way to spend Halloween," said Josh. "If we don't go trick-or-treating soon, people will start turning off their porch lights and we won't get anything. Peter's out there getting all the candy."

"Maybe he'll share it," said Jake.

"C'mon," said Wally. "I'm not going to wait a whole year for Halloween to come again."

"You guys give up too soon," said Jake. "They've *got* to come."

"Five more minutes, and then we go trick-or-treating," said Josh.

They waited. The wind picked up, and it grew colder still. And though Wally strained to see, there was no beam of light, no voices, no sound of leaves or footsteps, no snap of a twig.

"They've gone home," said Jake. "They *must* have gone home!"

"Or else they went over to Mary Ruth's and found out there wasn't any party," said Josh.

"Hoo boy, if *that* happened, they'll be ready to kill us," said Wally.

Jake jumped down off the wall. "Okay, I give up. Let's hit all the houses we can on the way back."

"You and your lousy ideas," grumbled Josh.

"You were in on it too!" Jake told him. "You helped choose the invitations. And you cooked the spaghetti, Wally, so don't blame it all on me."

"Don't remind me," said Wally. "What do we do with the spaghetti and worms?" He knelt down with the flashlight and lifted the lid on the saucepan. Then he gasped.

There was no spaghetti. No worms. Instead, there was a little piece of paper in the bottom of the pan, which read, *You boys come home this instant. Mom.*

Jake read it, then Josh.

"Oh, no! How did she find out!" said Josh.

"She must have missed her spaghetti. I *told* you we shouldn't have used the whole box, Jake!" Wally moaned.

"Are we ever going to catch it!" whistled Josh.

But Jake wasn't so sure. "Wait a minute," he said. "Think about it."

"I *am* thinking about it. We're in trouble," Wally croaked.

"Somehow this doesn't sound like Mom," Jake went on.

"Yes, it does," said Wally.

Jake shook his head. "Mom would say, 'You boys come home this *minute*.' Did you ever hear her say 'this *instant*'? And when she leaves us a note, she uses those little notepads from the hardware store, not a piece of yellow tablet paper. Also, she never prints, and *this* note is printed instead of written."

Wally looked at Josh, Josh looked at Jake.

"Them?" they cried.

"Them!" said Jake. "They're trying to ruin our Halloween. Somehow they found out what we were up to, and they figure we'll go right home, confess everything, and lose out on trick or treats."

Wally felt an enormous burden lifting off his chest. "Then we *don't* have to go straight home?"

"Of course not. Somebody's got to carry the pan, but there's still time to hit a lot of houses."

Wally carried the pan. They headed for the cemetery entrance, and the first row of houses just beyond.

"Where are your costumes?" one woman

asked them. "You boys don't look like trick-or-treaters to me." But she gave them candy anyway.

The pickings were slim, however. Some people had already turned off their lights. Some houses had run out of candy, and still others were down to little boxes of raisins or pennies. The dentist was even giving out apples instead of candy!

Desperate, they fanned out, trying to ring as many doorbells as possible. Sometimes, Wally knew, when you were the last one to come by, people dropped all the remaining candy in your bag, but it wasn't happening now, and he had to work twice as hard and run twice as fast to fill up even his pockets.

They met again on the corner, and by twenty after nine there were no more porch lights on anywhere. A policeman cruising by stopped when he saw them and rolled down his window. "You fellas better get on home now," he called.

Silently, glumly, Jake and Josh and Wally turned toward home, with barely enough candy to carry in their jackets. Mother always said that Halloween candy should last all year, and they'd hardly picked up enough to last through December.

"You know what I'm thinking?" Jake said as they turned up their street. "Maybe it's time we called a truce. I mean, just give up bugging the

girls. *Forget* about them. Find other guys at school
to hang around with. Whether the Malloys stay
here or not probably doesn't have anything to do
with what the Bensons decide. Those girls have
ruined enough things for us. This Halloween was
really the pits."

"I've been trying to *tell* you that," said Wally.
"I'm getting a little tired of 'The Malloys this . . .'
and 'The Malloys that. . . .' Everything we do,
practically, is connected to the Malloys."

"Okay," said Jake. "As of right now, we just
forget about them. They can go, they can stay, it
doesn't make any difference to us."

"I feel better already," said Wally, with a sigh.

"So do I," said Josh.

They went up the steps to the house.

"We should have done this long ago," said
Jake. "We're free! Back to boy-stuff again." He
smiled. Josh smiled. Wally smiled. They opened the
door.

There in the living room sat Eddie, Beth, and
Caroline in their costumes, as well as Peter in his
pajamas, a ring of chocolate around his mouth.

Mrs. Hatford hurried toward the boys. "Where
in the world have you been?" she asked, and for a
minute Wally thought she was going to sail right
past them and on out the door. "Why did you invite
these girls to a party and then not even have the

decency to show up? You didn't even *mention* it to me."

"A party?" cried Jake and Josh and Wally together.

But before they could say another word, the girls all chanted together:

> *"Little witch has come to say,*
> *Ghosts and goblins like to play.*
> *Won't you come and join the fun?*
> *There'll be treats for everyone."*

"Jake, I want you to take your money and run to the store for some Cokes or something. Josh, you're in charge of games," Mrs. Hatford said.

And as Wally watched helplessly, his mother took all the candy they had collected, dumped it in a bowl, and passed it around the room for starters.

About the Author

•

Phyllis Reynolds Naylor is the author of more than seventy-five books. She was born in Indiana, but her husband was born in West Virginia. She admits she has fallen in love with his state, and several of her books take place there, including *Shiloh*—which was awarded the Newbery Medal—*Josie's Troubles*, and *Send No Blessings*. Her most recent book for Delacorte Press was *The Boys Start the War*. Among other honors, she has received the Edgar Allan Poe Award from the Mystery Writers of America, the Christopher Award, the Golden Kite and the Child Study awards, as well as the annual book award from the Society of School Librarians International.

She and her husband are the parents of two grown sons, Jeff and Michael, and live in Bethesda, Maryland.